I0761855

TRANSCENDENT

LAREN RUBY

VIRGO RISING PUBLISHING
BIRMINGHAM, AL

This book is a work of fiction. Names, characters, places, and incidents are the product of the author's imagination or are used fictitiously. Any resemblance to actual events, locales, or persons, living or dead, is coincidental.

Virgo Rising Publishing

Birmingham, AL

Visit us at virgorisingpublishing.com

First paperback edition: October 10, 2021

The publisher is not responsible for websites (or their content) that are not owned by the publisher.

ISBN: 978-1-7379711-0-8 (Hardback)

ISBN: 978-1-7379711-2-2 (Paperback)

ISBN: 978-1-7379711-3-9 (ebook)

Printed in the United States of America

For my husband and 4 fur-kids without whom this book would have been completed two years earlier.

To my parents, who will try to put this on the fridge.

In memory of my Grandma, who encouraged me to fly toward my dreams.

Prologue

April 8, 2051

THE GYMNASIUM AT THE Darnall Army Medical Center in Fort Hood, Texas was outfitted with advanced surveillance equipment, including infrared cameras, which measured micro-fluctuations in the tiniest human muscles. In addition to allowing the select team of scientists and doctors to observe soldiers undergoing rigorous testing in real-time, the recordings allowed for second-by-second review of training sessions to detect the slightest change in a subject's physiological response to the powerful serum they'd volunteered to test.

At three a.m., you'd think any ordinary soldier would be fast asleep in their rack. Dr. Marielle Stevenson, however, had noticed some anomalies in the data being recorded in the gymnasium when it was supposedly shut down for the night. Tonight, after lights out, she'd quietly made her way back to the observation deck. If something was going on with the test subjects, she needed to know about it. Incomplete data led to costly—and potentially, deadly—errors. And this project was too important to the future of the U.S. Army to leave anything up to chance.

As a general rule "woman's intuition" was not an approved scientific observation method, and definitely was not a verifiable method for gathering data. For that reason alone, Dr. Stevenson was hunkered down behind a screen set for night light. Granted, the observation deck was set twenty-two feet above the gym floor, so light shouldn't filter down so far. In this case, Dr. Stevenson wasn't taking any chances that being discovered might change the behavior patterns of her test subjects.

She was very glad she'd dimmed the screen. While she could look over the top to see what was taking place on the floor below, she needed a recording of the off-schedule workout in progress for further review. Besides, she could see far more clearly the nuances of the activities being engaged in with her eyes barely inches from the screen. Nuances she would otherwise have missed, watching from so far above the floor.

She'd already determined that the soldiers engaged in the off-hours training session were from the 2719-GT group. She'd had her suspicions about this group from Week Seven. The twenty men and women who'd been given this version of the bio-enhancement serum had shown marked improvement in their overall fitness levels, as well as in cognitive ability, right through to Week Six. At that point, their improvement levels had dropped off to those recorded in Weeks Four and Five, without explanation.

Now, she had proof that these test subjects were faking their responses to the serum.

The huge gymnasium below was barely lit, only a few widely spaced emergency lights remaining on once the overheads had been turned off for the night. Yet the men and women of group 2719-GT were performing as if they were standing outside in full sun on the open training grounds.

Enhanced visual acuity, in addition to the physical strength enhancements and increased fine motor skills.

"My god," Dr. Stevenson barely breathed the words, watching the rigorous routines one subject after the other put themselves through in absolute silence, running, jumping, pulling themselves up and over a variety of treacherous obstacles set up in a *Sasuke* Ninja course, going all-out in the near dark, without hesitation or misstep. The times recorded on the surveillance equipment were fully twice what they'd averaged just three weeks ago. Serum 2719-GT was proving dangerously effective.

Dangerous being the operative word.

Marielle Stevenson had been having nightmares lately about her work on the Super Soldier project. Unlike the top brass, who saw only the opportunity to develop a military force able to far outstrip that of any other country on the planet, Dr. Stevenson was able to look beyond the immediate results. Women's intuition, again? Her dreams were filled with an elite cadre of superhumans who took over the world.

And the ordinary, untreated ones who served their superiors.

That was not a world she wanted to live in.

An anomalous biometric reading on one of the monitors caught her attention suddenly. Test subject 2719-GT-15 was running the course now, barely eleven seconds behind the team leader. 15's biometrics were something which was absolutely impossible. Not the physical superiority bestowed by the test serum...

Or at least, not *just* that.

Test subject 2719-GT-15 was pregnant.

Stunned, Dr. Stevenson sat back in the chair, tilting the screen downwards to further hide its dim light in the blackened observation deck. The implications for one of the U.S. Army's super-soldiers being able to procreate were terrifying. Every test subject was implanted with a hormone injection device that prevented conception. It was essential that these soldiers remained infertile during the testing process, for the safety of everyone involved.

What could the results be for a fetus exposed to the serum *in utero*? This was a true Frankenstein scenario.

Marielle knew this news couldn't wait until morning. She quickly copied the biodata into a file under the subgroup records for 2719-GT, and then emailed it to herself as extra insurance. Shutting down the terminal, she swung around in the chair and stood up silently, heading for the door. It might be nearly four in the morning, but General Lazerus needed to be told. Immediately.

But as she stepped out of the observation deck into the upper corridor, she stopped short. How did she not notice? Every member of 2719-GT was ranged throughout the corridor leading to the elevator, blocking her escape.

In that moment, she knew they'd let the extremely deadly genie out of its bottle.

And she wouldn't be around to help seal it back in.

Chapter One

June 1, 2312

DESPITE THE OBJECTIONS OF our Council of Elders, it seems that every Transcendent-aged kid in the community is clustered in front of the Lottery booth at Eie's yearly Community Harvest Festival. Even though most—all?—of them won't go to Mag City, they want to see what they're missing.

"I can't believe it, Kairyn," my best friend, Ulna, says, transfixed. The images playing out across the screen seem real enough to touch. If we reached behind the counter, could we feel the sweat on that warrior's brow? Could we feel the silkiness of the alpaca's hair? Could we shake hands with the very king of Elleon? "Are those people *really* real?"

I crowd closer to her, my hip bumping the counter as more people push in behind us.

"I think they are," I say, pointing at the middle of the three screens, the one directly in front of us. It shows a procession through the streets of Mag City, similar to our Harvest Festival. Similar, but so very different.

King Ilan and Queen Helena, hereditary *Lorem Sanguis* of Elleon, are accompanied by their son in a shining glass vehicle, driving slowly down a wide boulevard. Other officials—more *Lorem Sanguis*, descendants of the First Twenty— are in front and behind in their own vehicles, the sun glinting off the polished chrome. In between the motorized vehicles came ranks of uniformed warriors, Purple Bloods, men and women dressed in the Royal livery, along with exotic animals such as no one ever saw here in the outer communities.

"Well, those aren't real," Ulna says, indicating the ranks of screens set up to either side of the central one. "They look like...like... paintings."

"Those are video games, Miss," one of the Lottery officials steps up in front of us holding a black device with many-colored buttons. "If you enter the Lottery, you'll get to play games like these. Watch," she says, pointing the device at a screen on the left.

Her fingers pressing the buttons quickly, she makes the figures in the video game run through ruined streets, jump gaping holes in the pavement, and swing from metal bars above their heads. They scale the sides of crumbling buildings. They leap from rooftop to rooftop. And all the while, other figures chase them relentlessly.

Blue Bloods being chased by Purple Bloods, with those exotic animals caparisoned in matching armor. The Purples chase the

Blues like we do deer in the forest, with hunting dogs.

By the end of the demonstration, my heart is pounding, even though I haven't lifted a finger or a foot. I feel as if I've run miles, following in the character's footsteps. Is this my fate, and that of my Blue Blood friends? Will we be chased down through the grounds of the annual Transcendent Hunt?

Or will I be the one doing the Hunting?

The community of Eie's Council of Elders refuses to allow their young people to take part in the annual Lottery. In the 187 years since the Transcendent Campaign was established, not one person from our Blue Blood community has actually entered the Lottery.

Not as prey. Well, except for Year 83, but no one speaks of that.

"Of course, this is pretty low-tech," the woman says. "Your facilities here don't allow for a full set-up. If you get to Mag City, you'll really see something spectacular."

"Well, that's not ever going to happen," I say, mostly for Ulna's benefit.

We're so far from Mag City that no Purple Blood has been born here since Year 83. Mallen of Willow Creek was the first—and only—Purple Blood from Eie. And Blue Blooded kids are not encouraged to enter the Lottery. In fact, our Council of Elders *strongly discourages* that.

“My mother would never let me take part in the Lottery,” I say. “She says it goes against our values as a community.”

The woman shakes her head, turning away to speak to some other kids. All I can do is stare, entranced by the realism. And she says this is low-tech!

“But wouldn’t it be fun to play games like this?” Ulna has always been the most daring girl in our school, leading us in wild games of hunt and chase. Nothing like these video games, of course. “I’d love to go to Mag City, to compete in the Hunt. I’d win, I just know it! Just once, I wish we could be like the kids in other communities.”

Here in Eie—unlike the other eight communities making up the Transcendent Federation—we were taught from the time we could understand the concept that the Campaign was an evil thing, a thing of the Outside, and our lives were too pure to sully ourselves. We were Blue Bloods here. We didn’t submit ourselves to the Purples, not any more than the laws of Elleon decreed. Other communities saw the Campaign as a way to get ahead, to lift themselves up. We of Eie were taught to rely only on ourselves and remain apart from the brutality of those in Mag City, with all of their tech running their unhappy lives.

That tech, however, was what brought the teens of Eie flocking to the Transcendent Lottery booth at the festival. We'd never see anything tech, if not for this.

The crowds pushing in behind Ulna and me are growing. I grab her wrist and pull her after me, giving way to other kids eager to see the "video games." As we break through the edge of the crowd, my eyes meet those of my mother, Oma. She's standing silently under the widespread branches of a nearby oak tree, along with several of the other members of the Council of Elders, her hands tucked inside the sleeves of her Council robes.

She holds my gaze for long seconds. Too long. The look of disappointment on my mother's face crushes my heart.

Ulna follows my gaze and pulls me close into her side, whispering in my ear. "It's not like you're going to enter the Lottery," she says. "We were just looking. Know your enemy, right?"

I turn away from my mother's disapproving look, wrapping my arm around Ulna's waist. Best friends forever.

"Right," I say. "Even if we did, and won, I could never live in Mag City. No prize would be worth giving up everything that matters to me." I turn with Ulna and head down the packed-dirt street in the opposite direction. Even for a prize of a job and apartment in the capitol, a life of relative luxury, I would still be serving Purple Bloods as a glorified servant. "I mean, you wouldn't, would you?"

Please say no! Stay here in Eie. Stay safe.

Ulna has a dangerously confident view of herself, and of her abilities. She would be the one to think she could outwit the Purples and win a place in Mag City.

"Everyone there has tech, and it makes their lives so much better," Ulna says as we continue down the street. "Would it be so horrible to experience it just once?"

We wander through the booths set up for the Festival, looking at the beautiful things for sale. Here in Eie we are almost completely self-sufficient, refraining from trade except for absolute life-sustaining necessities. So, the chance to buy something beautiful—even if made locally, by one of our neighbors—is something I look forward to every year.

Time flies as Ulna and I examine intricately woven baskets with fanciful designs at one booth, and delicately embroidered linens at another. Utilitarian wares are available, too: carefully worked metal pots, fine ceramic plates and mugs, leather belts and pouches with chased designs embossed into the hide. I think we were just eight or nine years old when Ulna's father made each of us a wooden hope chest, hers carved with deer and butterflies, mine with a design of entwined vines and wild roses. My father died when I was little, so I had no one to provide the chest which would hold all the things I needed to set up my future home.

Ulna's father certainly wasn't obligated to provide such a valuable gift. He was just that kind of a man, devoted to his family and caring for everyone in his community, even a fatherless girl.

"Kairyn, what do you think of this?" Ulna says, holding up a length of cream-colored wool cloth with flecks of rose and blue woven in. "Wouldn't it make a lovely maternity tunic?"

My friend is far ahead of me in planning out her life. Ulna is nearly a full year older than me, so she's had that luxury. I was the last of my year to turn Sixteen, and even though no one has tested Purple in Eie since Mallen, we never count our blood before it's tested, as the saying goes. Yet, Ulna's so sure of her future. She's already decided who she wants to marry. She even has the plot of land picked out where she wants to start her farm and build her house.

"Is this for child number one, two, or three?" I ask, laughing.

Ulna's face drops. She can't understand how my hope chest is still half-empty, when hers will barely close. "You need to be more serious about your future," she says. "We don't have forever, after all. You've been Sixteen for a month now. In a year you'll be old enough to take a husband, and you haven't settled on anyone yet. If you wait any longer, the good ones will all be taken!"

"What if I don't want to be married?" I say. "What if I want more from my life than being a wife and mother, and running a farm?"

"Don't be silly," Ulna says, chiding. She is unable to see that there is anything outside of Eie, outside of our narrow lives. "Of course, you want to marry a handsome boy and have his babies. What else is there?"

As we move away from the woolens booth, I have to consider that. What else is there for any Eie girl? But the thought of such a narrow future, every day the same as the one before, just fills me with dread. Fills me with longing for something more. For something bigger.

These thoughts weigh heavily as Ulna and I spend the rest of the day moving through the Harvest Festival's many attractions, shopping, eating, playing games, and competing in the yearly race through the lanes outside the community, circling between the outlying farms. I hold myself back, a few paces behind my friend, allowing her to take the lead.

I am happy not to be the winner.

Winners have too many eyes on them.

Oma made me a pretty new tunic for the dance that night, and after I clean up and change into my new outfit, I walk down to the granary at the end of our main street, following the sounds of fiddles and drums.

The conversation I had earlier with Ulna still weighs on me. As I walk into the brightly lit barn, decorated with paper flowers and colorful chains of greenery, I look at my neighbors with new eyes. Was one of these boys meant to be my husband? No, that couldn't happen. If anyone was looking at me in that way, he was going to be disappointed. But must I be responsible for the future happiness of someone I hadn't promised myself to?

"Ryn! Ryn, there you are!"

I turn to find River, the son of our closest neighbor on Berry Lane, coming through the open barn doors. River is probably my best male friend in Eie. He never called me by my given name. He gave me the nickname Ryn when we were just toddlers, unable to say my full name. And that nickname has stuck with me, although only with him.

"River! Glad to see you bathed before coming," I say, reaching out to tousle his hair, still wet from the creek that runs beside his home. His dark brown hair was nearly black from the water. "You hardly smell of piss at all!"

He grimaces, but I smile to let him know I am joking. He's been pretty sensitive about his new job in the dyer's workshop. He's only been there a few months, so the nastiest job—collecting and transporting barrels of urine from around the community to the workshop, to be used as a mordant in the dying of cloth—has fallen to him. But despite how odiferous his job is, he is earning money to help support his mother and six siblings, so it is worth the smell.

Besides, he'll move up to apprentice dyer pretty soon, leaving the piss-hauling to some other poor kid. And dyer is a good job to have, enough to support a wife and children. Not that he has anyone in mind yet, either. We have that in common.

"You look...nice," River says.

I smile up at him as more of our neighbors crowd past us in the entry, eager to join the dancing in the barn. "You have a true gift for understatement, my friend," I say. "And here I thought I looked stunningly beautiful!"

I give a twirl in my new outfit, a knee-length woolen tunic split up the sides to show the lace-edged petticoat swirling around my ankles, both in shades of spring green. Ulna says that this is the perfect color to wear with my tanned skin, but I just think it makes me look like a sapling. Bark brown skin, brown hair, and green outfit.

I definitely look like a tree.

For just a moment, I flash back to what the people at the Lottery booth were wearing earlier. Unlike our hand-dyed, handwoven wool and cotton fabrics, they were wearing some kind of shimmery, silky-smooth cloth which clung to their bodies, showing every muscle and curve. Wearing something like that would be amazing. I'm glad those Mag City people never come to our community dances. I'd be ashamed to be seen next to them, even in a brand-new outfit.

"Would...would you like..." River is being stunningly tongue-tied. I wonder if he's hoping to meet some special girl here tonight and ask her to dance. If so, he'll never make the right impression if he hems and haws like this.

"'Would I like to dance?'" I say, taking the words he doesn't seem able to speak out of his mouth. "Why, yes, thank you, River. I would love to dance."

Luckily, my childhood friend is a lot more graceful with his feet than with his tongue. I'm glad to stand in for whatever girl he really wants to dance with, until he gets up the nerve to ask her. River is not a bad looking young man, really. A girl could do worse. Although he definitely needs to move up in the dyer's workshop as soon as he can.

No girl is going to want to go courting with a boy who often smells of piss, even when he's just bathed.

But after three dances with me, River doesn't seem inclined to ask anyone else onto the floor with him. He must have lost his nerve. He's never been very outgoing with the girls. In fact, he's never shown any interest in anyone, not that I know of. My feet are getting tired, however, and I pull away when he tries to lead me back onto the floor a fourth time.

"No more, River!" I say, laughing. "I'm getting overheated, and I feel a blister starting. Go ask someone else to dance. I'm going to get some fresh air." I turn my back and head for the doors, stopping abruptly when Alura, one of the girls who turned Sixteen last year, squeezes past me in the doorway. I haven't seen her since the previous year's Harvest Festival. She used to be the prettiest girl in Eie. Then her blood tested Red.

Very few of us tested Red, thank the gods. The treatments to turn her blood Blue like everyone else in Eie have hit her harder than most. It may be wicked of me, but I wonder how she even found the courage to come to the dance. No one is going to ask her onto the floor, even out of pity. I truly feel bad for her. I couldn't imagine being in that position. I shouldn't even think about that.

My eyes meet hers for the briefest moment and I turn away, ashamed of my reaction. But I know she saw the disgust I feel. She's not responsible. No one would choose to look like she does now, with bulbous growths on her neck and arms, and mottled skin rough as bark. Her right arm and left hand are twisted with muscle damage, unusable. But the treatments affect everyone differently. There's no way to predict what will happen.

I hurry to duck past Alura, stepping outside into the cool night air. The grassy area in front of the barn is lined with heavily laden refreshment tables, strings of lanterns hanging above to light the space.

I head for a table where cups of ice-cold plum cider are sweating in the warm air, only to turn and discover that River has followed me outside. I make a face, shaking my head.

"You're never going to find a girlfriend if you just follow me around all the time," I say. Looking at my friend, I wonder what would happen to his handsome face and straight spine if he tested Red and had to be treated for the condition. Or if Ulna did, or me.

I used to think living in Eie was the worst thing that could happen to one of us.

It would be a blessing, in fact, to test Blue tomorrow at the Transcendent Ceremony. The alternative—red—was unthinkable.

"I'm tired of dancing, too," River says, distracting me from my morbid thoughts. I know he's lying, though. He just didn't want to be left alone in the barn, where any girl could come up and talk to him.

I can't believe how awkward he is in social situations. "All right," I say. "We'll get a drink. But then you need to go back inside and ask someone to dance."

He hesitates, looking away into the night as if there's something hiding out there. River is not known for speaking up. He seems about to say something, his mouth opening and closing like a fish gulping for air.

"I'm tired of dancing," he says, finally.

He really needs to practice his conversational skills.

I grab a cup of cider for myself and hand one to River, who follows me to a bench set beneath the spreading branches of an oak tree on the outside of the green space.

He's never seemed like the bashful type, but I've never seen him with any girl. Or boy, for that matter. "I...I'm just thirsty," he says, draining his cup in one long gulp as if to prove his words. He sits down beside me, careful to leave as much space as possible between our thighs.

"You need to loosen up some," I say. "I'm sure there are plenty of girls in there who'd dance with you. Or boys, if—"

"No! I mean, no, I don't want to dance with anyone, only—"

"I never thought you were the shy type, River," I say. "How are you ever going to find a partner, if you won't even try talking to anyone but me?"

'I...I don't..."

"Hey, did you see those screens at the Lottery booth today?" I ask, remembering how thrilling it was to see the tech up close. "Don't you wish we could have something like that here in Eie?"

"The Elders would never allow that," he says. "And even if they did, the governmental authorities would never let the communities have tech that sophisticated. 'Only what is necessary to keep production of essential goods at current levels, or to exceed quota,'" he intones, repeating the primary rule we've been raised on.

"I know," I sigh. "But it would just be so much fun—"

River's snort would turn off any girl but me. And that's just because we've been friends since we were toddlers. "'A productive life is all the fun you need to hope for.'"

"If you're just going to quote the rules at me, I'm going back inside," I say.

"Wait...wait a minute. You're not...you wouldn't..." River has a real problem saying what he means sometimes, especially when what he wants is in opposition to me.

But I know where he's going. "Would I enter the Lottery? Take the chance of winning a place in the Transcendent Hunt?" I laugh, looking off into the darkness beneath the trees. As if that is even an option now. "Oma would never let me."

"She's right," River says. "It's not what we do. We don't need to be a part of that. All that tech. It just makes people wish for what they can't have."

"So, you'll be happy here in Eie, for the rest of your life, doing nothing but working and getting married and raising babies?"

"Well, yeah," River says. When I turn to look in his face, he's staring at the ground, turning his empty cup around and around in his hands. "With the right person, a girl I really loved. And who loved me."

He looks up into my face, into my eyes. The light is dim here beneath the trees, but I think I see something there that I've been doing my best to ignore for weeks. The way he looks at me has changed. And it makes me extremely uncomfortable.

"I hope you find her, then," I say. It may seem cruel, but I need to stop him before he can say something he can't take back. Something that could ruin our entire friendship. "Or him. Whatever your choice is."

"Ryn—"

"I'm going back inside," I say quickly, before this can go any further. "I promised Ulna I'd dance with her brother. I'll see you later."

It takes everything I have not to look back at the bench beneath the trees, and my friend. I can't bear to have that handsome face etched in my mind, the corners of his mouth drooping with disappointment, those soft brown eyes looking like a puppy someone has pushed away, refusing to love it.

I've known for a while now that River is in love with me. I tried to ignore it, but I have to face the fact that he wants to be with me. It breaks my heart to walk away and leave him sitting alone in the night.

Because, when all's said and done, I don't feel that way about him. And I never will.

Chapter Two

EVERYONE IN EIE IS required to attend the Territorial Governor's address, held the morning after the Harvest Festival dance in the same empty barn, still draped with drooping clusters of wilted greenery. Although Governor Larpidis arrived in Eie yesterday afternoon, he did not attend the Festival or the dance. Every year he claims he needs to rest after his long journey and stays in a metal caravan which arrives a few days ahead of him and is set up outside the cluster of houses which makes up our community.

The Elders say he doesn't want to associate with dirty Blue Bloods like us. Folk who work for a living, without tech, getting our hands dirty. If that's true, they say, we should be glad. We don't need the government coming here and messing with our way of life.

It's true. We are unsophisticated. Just look at us, sitting on folding chairs lined up in the village's storage barn, where until a month ago the year's production of woolen cloth was held until it was ready to ship out to the other communities. I bet the other communities have a real meeting hall to hold big events like this, not just a barn. A meeting hall, with electric lights and air-cooling machines and gas to cook their food instead of wood fires.

We've all heard rumors of the benefits other communities earn, sending kids to take part in the Transcendent Hunt. Just once in my life I'd like to try some of that tech. I'd like to walk into a room and flip on an electric light, instead of fumbling with a lantern or candles. I'd like to cook a meal in a gas oven, without ending up with ashes in my stew. I'd like to take a bath by turning on a faucet and having hot water flow out, and not have to haul bucket after bucket of freezing cold water from the well, and heat it in the kitchen fireplace, then bathe in a tin tub set beside the hearth. After the demonstration at the Lottery booth, I'd like to be the one who gets to play the games. They look like fun. And there definitely is not enough fun in our lives.

Our lives are all work and no play.

Is it so wrong to want to play sometimes?

"Good morning, People of Eie!" Our governor is a Transcendent, a Purple Blood of the elite class. The color of his blood is visible in the veins on his forehead. Deep purple lines run beneath his skin, so dark compared to the Blue Blooded adults I'm familiar with. The people of the communities, the Blue Bloods, with our sky-blue veins, are looked down on as unsophisticated and stupid by the Purples, despite the fact that we provide ninety percent of the goods, and one hundred percent of the food, that support all the people of Elleon. "I'm so very happy to be here with you again, in your most charming bucolic community."

Every word the governor speaks, it seems, is imbued with contempt for our way of life. As I look around at my Blue Blooded neighbors I am beginning to understand why. We are so backwards, so unrefined here in Eie. It's not just the lack of anything material, the lack of the tech devices which would make our lives so much easier. It's the way the people so openly despise the Purples, as if our Blue Blood makes us better in some way.

That is so obviously not the case.

Governor Larpidis goes on about our fine textile industry, the quality of our products, and the high output from our weavers. He speaks about how we are the backbone of cloth production throughout the territories, clothing the entire population of our communities. He even makes a joke about people going naked if not for Eie's fine cloth, which gains him some chuckles, but equal grimaces.

Eie is not known for its liberal views. And the joke is in pretty bad taste, really.

I notice that Governor Larpidis is not wearing Eie's fine woolens. His suit is made from Mag City cloth, so tightly woven you can't see the threads, rippling in the light with every move he makes.

It's hard to pay attention to the words he speaks, imagining myself wearing a tunic of cloth that fine. Until he gets to the part about Eie's lack of community spirit, never sending anyone to participate in the Transcendent Hunt. How we don't care about connecting with the other communities in this fun yearly event. How we think we're too good to send kids to participate. We could improve life for everyone if we allowed products from other communities within our borders, even Mag City tech.

Governor Larpidis is looking at our Council of Elders when he says these things, all of them lined up in the first row of chairs in front of the stage. They're all so smug, so full of themselves. Even my mother, sitting there with her face closed off, chin lifted, as if the governor was a little boy who could be cowed with a look.

I'm suddenly feeling stifled, as if there's not enough air in all of Eie to draw a deep breath. I jump up and push my way past the knees of my friends and neighbors, leaving them behind in the confines of the barn, of their narrow little lives. Slipping out the doors, I glance back at the stage where the Governor is still speaking, at the row of chairs directly in front of that stage. The eyes of everyone are on me, but I don't care.

I can't care.

I just need to get out of there.

"You, too?" Ulna is standing outside the testing tent in a cluster of other Sixteens. Everyone is dressed in their Testing outfits already. White tunics, thigh-length for the boys and below the knee for us girls. Soft white pants that tie at the waist.

Within just hours, our pristine white outfits will be marked with dyes in the colors of our blood. I can see that knowledge in the eyes of everyone clustered outside the tent. Knowledge we are afraid to admit. Our eyes slide aside from all the white, trying not to prejudge.

I have to wonder, though. How many of us expect to come out of the tent with blue stains on our clothes, and how many want purple? And which of us will be disappointed?

Governor Larpidis finally emerges from the barn, accompanied by the entire Council of Elders, my mother included. He climbs into a motorized cart driven by a Blue Blood from Mag City, one who had won a place in the Hunt years ago and now serves as the Governor's chauffeur. The Council of Elders follow behind the cart as Governor Larpidis sets off on his annual tour of Eie's industries, while the rest of the adults—and some of the older children—carry all those folding chairs out of the barn and set them up in ranks outside the Testing tent.

We Sixteens are silent as we watch them work, too nervous to talk to each other. River comes up to stand beside me, nodding at Ulna. Would Ulna be a good match for River? They've always been friendly. Maybe I should encourage them to get together.

I can't help but take note of the way the chairs were being arranged. Just like every year, the majority of chairs face the tent's opening, lined up in rows. But facing them—their backs to the tent—are twenty-three chairs on each side, separated by an aisle. Twenty-three chairs for this years' twenty-three Sixteen-year-olds. The ones on the left-hand side have blue ribbon rosettes draped from the backs, while the ones on the right-hand side have purple. As we each are given the serum which turns our blood to its permanent color from Red, are tested, and then sprayed with blue or purple dye to indicate our fate in this world, we will leave the tent and take a seat on the proper side.

Every year, there are an equal number of chairs on each side, Blue and Purple.

Each year, the Purple seats are left empty. They still have to be there, though. Just in case.

There are never any Red chairs.

I catch sight of Alura, standing off to one side under the same tree where I sat with River during the dance last night. She's with another former Red, an older woman. Like Alura, the gray-haired woman's face droops on one side, like a cake left out in the sun, sugar frosting melting down. But while Alura's right arm and left hand took the brunt of the damage to her extremities, twisted painfully out of alignment like gnarled tree branches, the old woman's serum damage was to her legs, both of them twisted like corkscrews so that she can't even walk. She's lived in a wheelchair since she was our age.

This is what happens when a Sixteen tests Red Blooded. When the regular serum doesn't reveal someone as Blue or Purple Blooded, they have to take the corrective serum. That's the one that destroys your body, even as it turns your blood to an acceptable color.

River sees me looking at the two women beneath the tree and steps closer. Leaning in, his voice is low. "Do you ever think—"

"No! No, don't even consider it," I say. Red Bloods are too rare to even think about. In the history of Eie, I think there have been less than ten, although other communities have had higher percentages than here. Another reason that our Elders don't want tech here.

They think it makes our blood susceptible to mutations like that.

"It's bad luck to look at them," Ulna leans in. "You shouldn't even acknowledge they exist. I couldn't stand it if I turned out—"

She shudders, unable to even voice the thought. Putting an arm around my shoulders, she forces me to turn and watch the chairs being set up, at the people taking their places. Everyone in Eie will be here for the Revelation ceremony, when we're presented to the community as Blue Blooded adults. Within minutes, a flap on the left side of the tent opens and a Purple Blooded doctor steps out.

"Welcome, Sixteens!" she calls out. "This is your big day. I know you're all excited, so let's get started. Single file, please! Everyone go on inside and find a cot. Yes, you can stay near your friends...No pushing! There's no hurry. Right this way."

River, Ulna, and I are the last ones inside. There are twenty-three cots, twenty of them already occupied. With an apologetic look at River, I follow Ulna to the two remaining cots which are next to each other, while River is forced to take the very last on the far side of the big tent. I can feel his eyes on me as I push up the long sleeve of my white tunic and lie back on a pillow. The cots are too far apart for Ulna and me to hold hands and reassure each other that we'll get through this day successfully. But we are close enough to talk as the Purple Blooded attendants put the serum needles into our arms.

Just as we've been told in our Transcendent lessons, the serum makes us cold, colder than walking outside naked in the wintertime. The attendants wrap us each up in heated blankets, but still we shiver uncontrollably. One by one, each of us Sixteens start to warm up again, a sign that the serum has done its work of determining our blood status. One by one, we Sixteens are led from our cots into the other side of the tent, where a sample is taken and placed under the microscope. One by one, we are sprayed with dye the color of our blood and led outside to the chairs in front of the tent.

I watch as others are led from their cots into the other side of the tent, the curtain dropping behind them. Kids from school. River. Then Ulna. In just a moment, I hear my best friend cry out, "No!" and then a scuffle on the other side of the tent, before things go silent again. It's several minutes before the attendants come for the last two boys, ones I barely know, and lead them out. I am the last.

I am alone.

What happened with Ulna? Did she test Purple? I begin to shake, thinking of life alone here in Eie, without my friend. But there's nothing I can do. No way to know until I step outside and see Ulna in dye-splattered clothing, in the Blue chairs.

Or the Purple ones.

It seems like forever before the attendant comes for me, helping me up from beneath the blankets and leading me over to the other side. Where throughout this whole process it seemed like there were dozens of technicians and doctors scurrying around, now there is only the head doctor, the one who welcomed us all into the tent earlier. Even the attendant ducks out of the tent after she seats me at the table where the doctor draws a sample of my blood and slides it under the eyepiece of the microscope.

But then my mother, Oma, slips in silently through an opening at the rear of the tent.

"Mom, what's going on?"

She exchanges a look with the doctor, who leans in to look through the microscope at my blood sample. Holding a finger to her lips for silence, Oma waits until—*finally*!—the doctor leans back in her chair, shaking her head.

"What? What is it? Mom—"

My mother nods to the doctor, who moves away to give us some privacy. "Kairyn, there's something I need to tell you. Something that's going to be very difficult for you to hear." Mom sinks into a chair beside mine, turning to look me straight in the face.

We must all meet the future head-on. That has always been Mom's favorite saying.

"What? Am I—" But I can't even say the words. My mind flashes to the scuffle I heard earlier. If Ulna is a Purple, will I be able to stay with her in Mag City?

My mother clears her throat. This must be so hard for her, a member of the Council of Elders. If her daughter is Purple...

"You are not my child by birth, Kairyn," she says bluntly, reaching out to hold my hand. "You were adopted from a mother in Mag City, who couldn't keep you. I know this is a shock." Her voice hardens. "I always knew that someday I would have to give you up."

I am numb, freezing again as I did when the serum was first injected into my veins. She's not my mother? Why wouldn't she tell me this before the testing? "Mag City. That means...am I... Purple Blooded?"

My mother's eyes drop to our clasped hands, and mine follow. I pull away suddenly, shaking off her touch. *My mother—*

Not my mother.

Oma.

"Yes," she says softly. "I'm afraid so."

Chapter Three

THE REST OF THAT day is a blur. The doctor returns when my mother—when Oma—goes to take her seat with the Council of Elders. I don't know how she will be able to look them in the eyes. The doctor hands me a card with my new Purple Blood identification number and information, sprays my clothing with purple streaks of dye, and leads me out of the tent.

Everyone in the audience falls silent, shocked. No one since Mallen of Willow Creek has tested Purple Blooded. And look how he turned out! What he did. They see me as a monster like him, I just know it.

Mallen of Willow Creek tested Purple Blooded in Year 83. And his boyfriend, Liiken—a Blue Blooded boy who'd been in love with him since they were fourteen—followed him to Mag City, entering the Lottery in hopes that he would win a place in the city and stay with his soulmate. Liiken thought his boyfriend would help him to win, so they could be together.

Mallen was the one who killed Liiken in the Transcendent Hunt.

The attendant leads me to the Purple chairs, where I sit alone, one girl on this side of the aisle, across from twenty-two other Sixteens.

Twenty-two Eie Sixteens who had the decency to test Blue Blooded. I don't see Ulna, but she must be there. Somewhere. River is in the front row of chairs, a stricken look on his face.

This is Mallen and Liiken all over again.

And then the ceremonies are over.

Governor Larpidis' chauffeur comes to escort me to the motorized vehicle, where I am told to sit in the front beside the driver. Even if I am suddenly a Purple, it seems I am still not up to our noble Governor's standards. I'm not allowed to return home for my things. I don't even have time to say good-bye.

Oma stands in the road behind as the vehicle pulls away, gaining speed and leaving her in a cloud of dust. I give a slight wave, pressing my palm to the glass, but she doesn't see it through the dark tinted windows.

I am numb.

It is evening when we arrive in Mag City. Throughout the hours of travel from Eie, Governor Larpidis ignored me, leaving me to the company of his driver. I sat entranced by the tech of the immaculate vehicle, silent, observing the lights and buttons and dials that Willet—for he told me that was his name, although he said little else—used to control the machine in which we rode. Governor Larpidis didn't even get out when we arrived at our destination but left it to Willet to escort me to the entrance of a huge building. The sun had set some time before, but it was as bright as day, with enormous electric lights every few feet along the streets, across the fronts of the buildings, and behind every window we passed.

Willet turns me over to a woman in a richly ornamented uniform who stands at attention, on guard outside the entrance. He says just two words: "From Eie." And then he is gone, too.

Everything and everyone from my former life has disappeared, and I am alone in the strangest of strange places.

Beneath the harsh white lights hanging above the carved wooden door of the building, which soars overhead with level after level of rectangular windows lit against the evening, the uniformed woman looks down her nose at me. That sharp nose wrinkles, as if I am River, reeking of piss from his job with the dyer.

But I am not River. I am Kairyn and I am a Purple Blood.

I still wear the evidence of that, if I just glance down to my formerly-white outfit, stained with dye from the ceremony that changed my fate in this world. I don't know what to expect now, but I know that I belong here, in Mag City. And I am not going to allow these Purple Bloods to shove me around from place to place with no explanation.

“What happens now?” I say to her, this Purple Blooded guard.

She tilts her head to one side, smirking. “Full of yourself, aren’t you, country cow?”

My chin lifts as I stare back at her. “I never wanted this. But now I’m here. Where do I go?”

I can read in her eyes that she’s about to say something cutting. Before she can get the words out, however, the door swings open on oiled hinges with barely a whisper of sound. She snaps to attention, her fist thumping the ornamented breastplate on her chest. A golden-skinned young man steps out, his own uniform stark black, his dark brown hair and brown-black eyes giving him a severe look. The guard takes a sharp step back, pivots on her heel, and marches away into the shadows.

Leaving me alone with another stranger.

As soon as the guard is gone, the young man’s stiff posture relaxes as he exhales with a *whoosh*. I look up in surprise to find him grinning. “Welcome to Mag City, Kairyn.”

“How...how do you know...”

His grin eases into a warm smile, which gives him a gentle look. Suddenly, I want to break down in tears, to crawl into Oma's arms while she rocks me in the old wooden chair beside the kitchen hearth fire and sings me baby songs filled with nonsense and love. But Oma is far away. Too far. I miss my home. My mother. My friends.

He sees my distress, this severe yet handsome young man, stepping forward to put a hand on my Purple-dyed shoulder. "It's easy to forget that people of the outer communities don't have much tech. Your Governor Larpidis reported that Eie had produced a Purple Blood, that he was bringing you in for decontamination."

He's felt my body stiffen, his hand still on my shoulder. His hand drops away and he steps back. First my own people, shocked into silence when they saw the Purple dye on my clothes. Then Governor Larpidis, ignoring my presence as if I were some farm animal invading his pristine vehicle. The guard calling me a cow. And now this.

Every Purple hates us. Hates me. Hates any hint of the communities.

"I'm not some filthy beast! We do take baths in Eie, for your information," I say to this young man in black. "I never asked to come here, and you—"

He holds up his hands in a placating gesture. "I'm sorry! Honestly. I didn't mean it that way." He steps back, shaking his head. "We should be more respectful, I know. Here, in the barracks, things are rather rougher than you're used to in Eie, in some ways. We're soldiers. We speak harshly, make jokes. But it's all an attempt to get through the training. Nothing personal. Let's start again."

He turns and walks back to the door, pulling it open and stepping behind the heavy wood panel before immediately stepping out again, the shiny metal ornaments on his chest flashing a reflection from the electric lights. He crosses the few steps to where I still stand, my mouth hanging open, and sticks out his hand.

"Greetings, Kairyn, and welcome to Mag City," he says, smiling widely. "My name is Xandyr Krim. I'm going to be your sergeant here, while you're in Basic Training."

I stare at the outstretched hand, as he reaches a few inches farther and grabs my hand to shake it up and down. "Not exaggerated at all." I roll my eyes. "But tha...thank...you?"

"Good!" His grin widens. "Perfect response! Now, you must be tired and hungry. Let's get you settled in for the evening. Training starts in the morning, and you want to be sharp."

"What...what do I call you?" I ask as he pushes open the door again, leading me inside.

"Krim is fine. Or Sarge. We're casual here in the barracks. But on the training ground, I'm a monster. Or so I've been told."

As we move inside the building there are more people milling around, many more. Sixteens, like me, looking either scared or awed. Some are still in their own freshly-dyed whites. Each one has a black-uniformed escort like I do, although when I look closer, I see that they don't have the same number of metal bits ornamenting their breast pockets as Krim does. A sergeant must have a higher rank than...whatever they are.

In Eie, we are a simple people, living simple lives. We are taught to never want more than what we have. After all, none of us ever test Purple, so longing for more than a country life is pretty foolish. But that doesn't mean we don't hear talk of life as a Purple in Mag City.

The Purple Bloods are the Chosen Ones. They are set above us Blue Bloods to protect and guard us, to keep us safe. In return, the Blues of the communities provide for their needs, tithing a portion of everything we produce to support them.

That means that every Purple Blood lives in luxury, in rich homes filled with tech to save time and energy for more important things. Those important things include compulsory military service for a prescribed term, to earn their place in society.

Compulsory military service. That means that I, a newly-tested Purple Blood, and all of the other fresh Purples I see wandering around the building Krim leads me through, must serve.

Must learn to fight.

Must take up weapons and prove ourselves.

Krim leads me up a flight of stairs and across a polished stone floor to an office, where black-uniformed Purple Bloods punch buttons on a flat thing with letters, those letters appearing on a screen very much like the ones we saw at the Harvest Festival Lottery booth. Was that only yesterday?

Once again, my heart clenches, squeezing until I can hardly breath. My vision begins to go black around the edges—

"Kairyn. Kairyn!" Krim is hissing at me, and reaches back to where I've stopped moving, stuck inside the door blocking others from walking. "Just a little farther," he says. "In here."

He leads me through another door, into a quieter room with long tables and benches. There are fewer people here, six or seven Sixteens and their guides, sitting spaced widely as the white-clothed new Purples eat. Or try to. Krim pulls me to a place at one of the tables, leaving me there while he grabs a metal tray and heads for a counter laden with stacks of plates and bowls. He loads the tray and returns quickly, sliding the food in front of me.

"Eat," he says. "That's an order." But he smiles when he says it and I pick up a fork, stabbing it into a pile of something white and fluffy. Potatoes, but prepared unlike anything I've ever eaten before. Green things, orange things, brown things. I know these are familiar foods, but the way they've been cooked is strange, everything flavorless and bland.

Or maybe it's just the fact that my life has changed into such a strange thing that nothing will ever seem familiar, ever seem right, again.

"If you'll give me your identification card," Krim says as I chew the tasteless food, "I'll go and get you logged in."

The card has been in the pocket of my tunic since I left the testing tent, and when I pull it out, I see a smear of purple dye has tainted one corner of the white paper. Tears fill my eyes against my will. I can't stop them from falling.

I am a Purple Blood now.

A glance at Krim and I know that he would comfort me if it didn't go against military protocol. It's in his eyes. Sympathy. I wonder if he came from a community, years ago. Or was he born here, a hereditary Purple Blood, born into this world and always knowing what to expect from his life?

He leaves me for a few minutes, my card in his hand, and returns with a sheaf of papers laid on top of a pile of gray clothing.

Others there in the room, eating at the long tables, have piles beside them as well. We are all the same now.

We are Purple Bloods.

We are soldiers.

Or we will be, too soon.

After my tray is emptied, Krim leads me through a big room filled with row after row of beds, each one tightly made up with a blue blanket on top of the sheets. We pass into a smaller room at the back with fewer beds. Beds covered with purple blankets. All but one of the beds is claimed, and Krim directs me there. The other Sixteens—all of us new Purples—sit or lie back on the beds, waiting for someone to tell us what to do.

We don't have long to wait. After conferring briefly with a young woman in the black uniform, Krim clears his throat.

"All right, then," he says loudly, his voice carrying to all corners of the room. We all look at him expectantly. "This is it. This is your home for the period of your training. Remember, at all times, you are Purple Bloods now. You have a job to do, and a position to uphold. And you will do it to the very best of your ability.

"I am Sergeant Krim, your lead instructor for Basic Training. This is your barracks." He indicates the room we are in, then points to the larger room we just came through. "That is the Blue barracks. You will live with the Blues while you train, but you will not fraternize with them. As you all know, Blue Lottery winners are your prey. You live with them, you train with them. You evaluate them for weaknesses and flaws. You learn how they think and how they react. And when the Transcendent Hunt begins, you will do your damnedest to kill them."

I am frozen, sitting on the edge of my cot. I knew this was coming, in the back of my mind. But I didn't want to admit it. Purple Bloods' compulsory military service requires them to fight for Elleon. But we have no enemies, outside of ourselves.

We make the Blues our slaves, our servants, and our enemies. This is why a Purple Blood never goes home again.

By the test, we have become monsters to our families, to our friends.

"Now, this year, for the first time in many years, we have an exceptional recruit. Many of you are familiar with the story of General Mallen, Purple Blood from the community of Eie. This year, another of Eie's finest Sixteens has tested Purple. I want you all to meet Kairyn."

My head snaps up as all eyes turn to me. As I look from face to face, I see many things. Things I don't want to see. Awe. Fear. Hatred. I wish Krim hadn't drawn attention to me like this. Not so soon, at least.

"Kairyn comes with a burden, and a legacy. Will she surpass you all? Will she live up to the example of her famous forebear? Only time will tell. But she's the one to watch, as your training begins."

My face is burning. My eyes are burning. If I had a knife, I would plant it in the heart of the one person I know in all of Mag City, twisting it until that organ popped free of his chest and I could crush it under my heel.

Sergeant Krim, my commanding officer, has just painted a purple target on my back.

I will never forgive him for this.

And when he's gone, when we've all changed into our night grays and crawled between our sheets, weighed down by purple blankets, the lights dimmed and eyes are supposed to be closed in sleep, the whispering goes on.

Beneath my blanket no one can see my tears.

Chapter Four

"ALL PURPLES TOGETHER!"

The cook standing behind the counter in the mess hall—for that is what I've learned that the big room where we eat is called—swings a ladle as he directs us from serving line to table.

"Your prey will be arriving later today. Don't think they want to be sharing their meals with the same ones who's gonna try to kill them in a few weeks, now, do ya?"

From the number of empty tables—and our single one, filled with trainees in gray uniforms—there will be five or six times as many Blue Lottery winners as there are new Purples. I know that adult Purple Bloods take part in the Hunt as well, and members of the military forces and the Royal Guard. Even so, the odds...

I dread even thinking about the Lottery, and the Hunt to come. No one from Eie takes part in the Lottery, or at least no one has in decades. I'm glad for that mercy. The thought of being forced to Hunt down and kill a member of my community, or being killed by someone I grew up with, is horrendous.

Like Mallen killed Liiken. The thought makes me shudder.

After breakfast we are marched out of the barracks and through what turns out to be an extensive training complex. There are fields where running tracks are laid out, obstacle courses, and exercise yards, where people in purple clothes are practicing hand-to-hand combat or using staves to attack each other. Our marching isn't very good, with people lagging or breaking ranks to stop and watch the adults training. I try to keep the cadence of the steps Sergeant Krim calls out, even though I, too, want to hang over the fences and watch the Purple Blooded adults dancing around the field, taking swipes at each other with electrified batons.

Finally, our disorderly ranks reach a stadium, where we file through a tunnel onto an open, oval field. Many of the seating sections are already filled with Purple Blooded spectators. In our communities, we are raised on tales of the Transcendent Lottery Day ceremonies but seeing the actual crowds of people from throughout Mag City all gathered together is overwhelming.

Are there really this many Purple Bloods? Or does it just seem that way, with all of them here together? I've never been anywhere but Eie, where our entire population would be lucky to top five thousand people, including all of the outlying farms.

We take seats in a roped-off section beneath the cloudless early morning blue sky. Below us, on the open field of the stadium, ten blue satin banners hang from poles, the names of the ten outer communities emblazoned upon them. Silver fringe waves along the edges of the banners, flapping gently in the breeze. It all looks so festive.

Sergeant Krim takes a few minutes to speak with a woman in uniform, one with more stripes on her shoulder than he has, then steps up in front of us where we sit. His head is below us, but he doesn't seem to strain as he looks up at where we sit, spaced out in the stadium seats.

He stares at us, each in turn, then finally shakes his head in a dramatic show of disappointment. "I must say, Purple recruits, that I have never in my career seen such an abysmal display as I did just now." He pauses, as if searching for words. But it feels to me as if this is all for show. "You do know that you are joining the ranks of an extremely privileged few, that you are the future rulers of Elleon? Because you certainly didn't demonstrate it just now. If you intend to train and fight as well as you just marched over here, then we might as well throw in the towel right now."

He pauses again, turning his back to us, staring out over the oval field in the center of the stadium. Shaking his head regretfully, he turns back to us. He reaches for the holster at his waist and slowly pulls out his handgun. I've never seen a gun in real life before, although there are pictures of them in our history books. Guns used to be freely available to all. Now, however, only Purples have the right to carry them. To use them.

He holds his gun up in front of him, squinting as he points the barrel at us, sighting down its length. Drama, again. Sergeant Krim steps closer to the front row of seats, suddenly flipping the gun backwards so that he is holding it by the barrel, the handle waving in front of a boy in the closest seat.

"Here," the sergeant says, "take it. Take it and put it to your temple and blow your brains out. Because if you people aren't willing to work harder to learn the skills I have to teach you—including marching in tight formation—then you might as well end your miserable lives right now. I've got plenty of bullets. End your suffering right now."

Everyone is shocked, speechless. We're barely breathing. I wonder if the Purple spectators are seeing this.

Surely, he can't mean it. Just because we didn't march over here in tight formation? Something he hasn't even taught us yet?

But he's not done yet. "If you aren't willing to train with every ounce of strength and will that you possess, you might as well end it now. Because your adversaries will be fighting with everything they've got. They are not going to lie down in the dirt and let you finish you them off. They are fighting to the death, so you'd better be ready to kill them."

Sergeant Krim flips his gun back around, grabbing it by the grip, and slamming it back into his holster. He crosses his arms over his chest and stands there in silence for a long moment, again looking each of us in the face. I shiver at the coldness in his eyes before his gaze moves to the boy next to me. Finally, he speaks again.

“My job as your commanding officer is to keep you alive long enough to reap the rewards of life as a Purple Blooded member of Elleon’s ruling class. If I do my job well, and you do yours, then we’ll get along fine. And your job starts now.” He turns his torso halfway around, pointing across the stadium to another wide tunnel opposite the one we entered through. “That is your enemy,” he says, as the tunnel fills with other kids from the provinces, a trickle at first, and then a flood. “Those are the Sixteens who entered the Lottery. The drawing takes place in a few hours, to determine which of those Blue Bloods will be given the opportunity to die at your hands, ensuring your place in society. And which of those Blue Bloods will end your lives, gaining wealth and fame in their home communities.”

What I wouldn’t give to be back in Eie right now, hoeing the weeds from the garden, feeding the chickens, picking apples in the orchard. Sweeping the kitchen floor while Oma washes the dishes. Sitting by the fire reading aloud while Oma sews a new quilt for my bed. Tears spring to my eyes at the thought of being safe in Eie, of never leaving.

I wanted more than to be married to a farmer, raising babies. But I never wanted this.

I never wanted to be forced to fight for my life.

Sergeant Krim turns back around, facing us. "I will train you to stay alive," he says, his voice dropping. Even though those kids are the width of the field away, they are staring at us. They must know what our Sergeant is saying. "But it is my job to train all of you, Purple Bloods and Blue Bloods alike. You will only triumph over your adversaries by being better, by being faster and stronger and more ruthless. This is an even playing field. You just need to play smarter than them if you want to stay alive."

With that, he turns and leaps over the guardrail separating the seats from the field, striding off to the top of the oval where a podium has been set up on a carpeted platform. There are chairs set out there, beneath an awning. Sergeant Krim takes his place with others in military uniforms, standing ramrod straight with perfectly stiff posture, just as a fanfare sounds. We crane our necks and look down to see our first Royal procession entering the stadium.

Although everyone in Elleon knows our ruling family by sight, from the official portraits hung up in every village hall and schoolroom throughout the country, few outside of Mag City have ever seen them in person. They are too busy—and too important—to travel to the small communities in the outlying provinces. This is as close as I have ever been to Royalty.

Accompanied by officials in governmental purple robes, embellished with silver and gold embroidery, the Royal party rides into the stadium in open-roofed motorized carts. The carts gleam deep purple in the sun, throwing flashes of light into our eyes as they pass in front of our seats. The procession enters through the double doors beside our section and circles in front of us, then around the stadium to the far side, in front of the Blue Bloods, finally pulling to a stop behind the awning.

We watch avidly as King Ilan and then Queen Helena are helped down from their cart at the edge of a purple carpet, led across the expanse to the edge of the platform, and then guided up a short flight of stairs. Our Purple Blooded king and queen join hands and walk to the front of the platform, as everyone in the stadium leaps from their seats and breaks into loud applause.

After a few moments the applause dies down, and we all take our seats again. Queen Helena steps back and sinks gracefully into a chair in the first row of seats, while King Ilan steps behind the podium.

"Welcome, Sixteens," he says solemnly into the microphone, fiddling with the position to get it just right. "This is the most important time in your young lives, and the most important time of year for everyone in the kingdom." He pauses to smile, as if to reassure us all that what we are doing here means something. I wonder what that meaning really is. All of this suddenly seems somehow barbaric, the pomp, the ceremony, the entire ritual. Is it really necessary?

I try to pay closer attention as the king continues with his speech, and to put my own thoughts aside.

"While we are all bound by the constraints of our blood types, we determined as a society that it behooved us to find a way to allow those of inferior blood to make their mark in our glorious society. Our forefathers devised an equitable way for Blue Bloods to reach beyond their station in life, to achieve greatness, to compete with their betters and win acclaim. And thus was the Transcendent Hunt born. All of you here today, Purple and Blue Blooded Sixteens alike, have the chance to better yourselves, to achieve greatness, through fair and equal competition. I am honored by your sacrifice, for the betterment of our society, just as I and my dear wife Queen Helena sacrificed in our own Sixteenth year to become your Royal family. I look forward to seeing what a stellar group of competitors we have this year, and to rewarding the victors at the end of the Transcendent Hunt!"

The king's speech finishes to thunderous applause. He steps back and holds out a hand to the queen, raising her from her seat. She takes his place at the podium and readjusts the microphone to her lesser height.

"Thank you, my love," she looks back at the king with a warm smile. Even from here, I can see that her smile doesn't quite reach her eyes. "We are about to begin the Lottery drawing, but first I wish to thank our competitors for their participation." She bows her head toward the Blue Bloods sitting in the section across the field from us. "Your sacrifice allows our society in the great kingdom of Elleon to continue to flourish, providing rewards for all those brave enough to claim them."

As she speaks, I can't help but think of those not brave enough—or lucky enough—to survive the Transcendent Hunt. Yes, those Blue Bloods who win through to the end walk away with a life of luxury guaranteed to them, with a good job here in Mag City. But they never return to their home communities, even though they send back parcels of city goods to enrich their families' lives.

But what about those who don't survive the Hunt? Is it really worth the Sacrificial Stipend paid to their families each year when they are dead and buried?

It's no wonder the Council of Elders in Eie refuse to allow any of the Sixteens to enter the Lottery. It's a barbaric custom. And even in her ceremonial royal robes, embellished with pounds of embroidery in gold thread, and a glittering crown atop her coiffed head, Queen Helena is as barbaric as the rest of these Purple Bloods.

And now I am one of them.

"And now it's time to proceed with the Lottery drawing," the queen says as an attendant rolls a polished silver box enameled with the royal coat of arms in deep purple up beside her. Above the coat of arms, the name of the first village is etched into the metal. A row of other attendants line up behind the first, each with their own box, each with the name of a different village.

With a flourish, Queen Helena shakes back the draped sleeve of her ceremonial robe and pulls a card from deep inside the first box. "Marcon Geddi," she announces the first name drawn. With a shout, a Sixteen boy leaps from his seat and pushes past the others in his row to reach the aisle where he is guided down onto the field. He stands there alone in front of the Eos banner, but only briefly, as the queen draws other cards, three from each village. One boy, one girl, and one random.

As more communities' participants are drawn, seats in the Blue Blooded section begin to empty out. Attendants with silver boxes move offstage as their village's competitors have been chosen. Small clusters—three each—form in front of the blue banners on the field below us.

Elm. Fen. Zag.

Eos. Kel. Oln.

Abi. Het. Qui.

Lottery participants from nine out of the ten communities in outer Elleon have been drawn. But then a final attendant steps up beside the queen. From my seat I can see the name of my village engraved above the royal coat of arms on the front of her box. Eie. But Eie doesn't participate in the Transcendent Lottery.

Maybe it's all for show.

Queen Helena reaches into the box. Her hand should be empty. When she pulls her hand from the box, though, there is a card in it.

There can't be a card from Eie.

No one from Eie would—

Frantically, my eyes range over the remaining Blue Bloods in the stadium section across from us. I don't see anyone from my village. It must be a mistake or an act. Maybe they don't want to let anyone know that Eie doesn't take part in this barbaric ritual, so they draw a card from another community, saying that it's someone from Eie.

The queen's voice rings out across the field, enhanced by the microphone so that it echoes through my bones. "River Pell."

"This concludes all of this year's lottery winners," she says while closing the box. I am frozen to my core. River. He followed me? I miss the rest of her closing speech with each passing thought

River has risen from a seat behind a hulking boy, whose bulk hid my lifelong friend from view. He stares across the field at me as he slides down the row of seats into the aisle, then is led down to the field. When River reaches the Eie banner, he stands there, not facing the platform where the king and queen are but turned toward me. Looking directly into my eyes.

How could he?

How could he enter the Lottery? How could the Elders allow that to happen?

Only a few days ago, we were at the harvest dance, and he wanted—

And I stopped him—

And now he is here.

It truly is Mallen and Liiken all over again.

Chapter Five

WHEN THE CEREMONY IS over and King Ilan and Queen Helena leave the stadium, along with their ministers and courtiers, Sergeant Krim takes the microphone and orders us Sixteens—both Purples and Blue Lottery winners—to remain while the rest of the audience files out of the stadium. The last to leave are the Blue Bloods who weren't selected in the Lottery. They will remain in Mag City, being trained for menial jobs in the homes and businesses of the elite Purple Bloods.

No one who enters Mag City seems to leave, for one reason or another.

Finally, it's just us new Purple Bloods in the stands, and the Blue Blood Lottery winners on the field. Sergeant Krim orders us down onto the grass then, where we take up positions opposite the row of banners.

It seems that we Purples instinctively took our places opposite the banners of our home villages, facing the kids we grew up with. I wonder if my fellow Purples feel as I do, that this is wrong. We shouldn't be fighting against our former friends and schoolmates.

This entire system seems so arbitrary.

I realize now that I have been extraordinarily privileged, growing up in Eie, where our Council of Elders strongly discourages participation in the Transcendent Hunt. I didn't grow up suspicious of my peers, separated from them, a wall of possibilities between us. Granted, there is always the uncertainty of how the Testing will go. But we never had to face the knowledge that someday we might meet our former friends in the Hunt.

All of the new Purples ranged to either side of me now on the stadium field have lived under that threat their entire lives.

"From this moment on," Sergeant Krim takes up a position between the two lines of Sixteens, pacing back and forth, "you will train together. You will live together. You will eat, sleep, and shower under the same roof. In the barracks, you will co-exist peacefully. But from this moment on, you are sworn enemies. There will be no fraternizing. There will be no personal attacks. There will be no bullying.

"That does not mean, however," he says slowly, emphasizing each word with a slash of his hand through the air, "that there will not be intimidation." He reaches the end of the facing lines and pivots smartly on his heel, retracing his steps. "You are equals in my training camp. You are each given the same tools, the same weapons, the same training to defeat your opponents. You will take full advantage of every opportunity given to you to decipher your enemies' strengths and weaknesses, so that when you reach the field of combat, you each will have the same chance of winning or losing, of living or dying. The Transcendent Hunt is not a game. It is how you earn a future in Elleon society, or how you end up in an unmarked grave."

My eyes reach across the grassy strip of ground between Blue Lottery winners and Purple recruits. River is staring directly into my eyes, a sad smile quirking the corners of his mouth upwards. Why is he here? Why is he doing this?

All of his life, River has been the boy in our year most likely to stand up for another kid, to step in and protect someone weaker than him. He never says much, but he doesn't need to. He goes straight to the point, saying what he means and leaving no doubt of his position. Except when it comes to girls.

River is totally unfit for the Hunt. While others measure and weigh, seeking ways around, behind, or underneath, River will plow forward without hesitation. He'll have a target painted on his chest from the very first training session.

An easy kill.

How am I supposed to keep him alive?

"From this point on," Sergeant Krim has returned up the invisible line drawn between our two sides, stopping in front of me, "you will do your best to meet my standards for military discipline, or you will pay the price. The Transcendent Hunt takes place in one month. I expect each and every one of you to perform to the highest possible degree."

He takes up a stance, facing us Purple Bloods with his feet spread, planting his weight on the ground. "Purples, I expect to see every single one of you back here on this field when the Hunt is over, breathing." He swings around and mirrors that sturdy stance, facing the Blues. "And I expect the same of you Blue Bloods." He pauses, turning to walk to the end of the lines nearest the doors leading out of the stadium on the Purples' side, facing away from us. "Fall in!"

Somehow, we manage to do it, shuffling into two lines behind the sergeant's steel-straight back. River is directly beside me in the line, and I allow my eyes to shift in his direction, looking up at him. He smiles at me, and my stomach turns over. Swallowing quickly, I force the vomit which threatens to spew out back into my stomach. I face front again, straightening my own shoulders and slapping my feet together as I have seen Krim do.

My training begins now.

Our lives in the barracks quickly settle into a routine. Four meals a day, Purples served first at breakfast and dinner, Blues served first at lunch and supper, the last meal of the day. Sergeant Krim is in charge of our daily lives, but he has subordinate corporals to relay his orders and to maintain discipline in the barracks. We quickly become used to the lack of privacy in the barracks, boys and girls sleeping in the same dormitories, and showering in the same washrooms. Some of the recruits from the farthest-flung communities have a problem getting used to this at first, coming from places where nudity is frowned upon. But for the rest of us, it's life as usual, growing up in communities with unisex bathhouses. There are some problems in the first few days, when a couple of the lottery Blues refuse to shower with members of the opposite sex in the same room, but the corporals quickly put an end to that, punishing them by making them stand along the walls during meals watching the rest of us eat, and getting nothing but bread and water themselves.

With the quality of the food we're given—the luscious hot meals and amazing desserts, and as much as we want of everything—the miscreants quickly give in and get past their modesty. It smells a lot better in the barracks after that. I'm thankful the food tastes much better than when I first came here. My foul mood must have caused the food to taste bland.

After breakfast each day we are assigned to different training courses. Over the coming four weeks, we need to hone our natural talents, and also learn new skills to allow us to defeat our enemies in the Hunt. These training courses are widely varied, from physical to cerebral. Sergeant Krim says we need to be able to think as well as we fight in order to win.

And losing is not an option.

Hand-to-hand combat training with staves, clubs, and weighted chains takes place in a large gymnasium. There are padded mats spread across the wide-open floor where we practice strikes, blows, and throws which leave everyone aching. In the showers, it's clear to see who is the slowest to learn, or the clumsiest at training, by the mass of purple-yellow-black bruises they sport across rib cages and legs.

There are also classes in weaponless fighting, using only hands and feet to attack our opponents. We line up in rows in the same gymnasium to learn stances, punches, and blocking techniques derived from some ancient forms of fighting. These have the strangest names: *Karate*, *Kung Fu*, *Krav Maga*, *Jujitsu*.

Weapons training with guns, like the one Sergeant Krim pulled on us the first day in the stadium, take place in an outdoor firing range where we shoot at targets of human outlines on paper. Once we score high enough on the paper targets, we begin to practice on a special course set up in an enclosed area, where we wind through a maze of rooms and corridors, and targets pop up from the floor or from behind walls. There are both Purple and Blue targets, and if we shoot the wrong ones—the Purples, of course—we lose points. We also practice with long-range rifles and automatic weapons which fire dozens of bullets in seconds, spraying them across a wide area to mow down everything in their path. For practice with those weapons, they bus us outside the city into the hills, where we fire at targets set up in the forest or on the tops of far-off hills.

We also have classes in tactics, studying battles from past military campaigns, concentrating on what the instructors call "gorilla warfare." Apparently, gorillas were monstrously huge animals which attacked humans thousands of years ago, but they were all wiped out in human wars.

And—finally—we get to play those simulated reality games like we saw at the Harvest Fair booth back in Eie. But—as the woman at the booth told Ulna and me—it's far more realistic than what we saw on that screen.

Each of us is assigned to a small room, about ten feet square, where we practice alone. Wearing a heavy black helmet that fits over our eyes, we watch a scene appear, similar to where we train in the real world. One setting is an abandoned building, where we run through room after room, down corridors, up staircases, or repel down deep shafts, all using just the controllers embedded in the special gloves we wear. Another is set in a jungle, which is similar to the real forests we go to, but with more treacherous terrain and dangerous animals. The jungle is filled with giant snakes, enormous wildcats, and attacking birds with massive wingspans. The foliage is so dense that we can't see three feet in front of us. There are ravines, towering cliffs, rushing rivers, and treacherous pools of quicksand. The views are so real, that I often forget it's not and that I can turn it off at any time.

Once we're used to the standard settings, we're given weapons to use as we traverse the virtual settings. These weapons act like the real thing, in the games at least. While they slice through the bodies of giant snakes and impale monstrous saber-tooth cats in the headsets, in the real world—in the rooms where we practice —the dull blades bash harmlessly off the battered wooden walls, scarred from past classes of recruits training there. When we fire fake guns, no bullets rip through the world around us, only points of light.

Even with all of the training they put us through so that we can survive the Hunt, we still have a few hours free in the evenings before lights out when we are able to socialize, getting to know our teammates, as well as our opponents. We gather in a large common area of the barracks to play games of chance and skill like chess and *Arimaa*, to listen to music, or to watch programs about life in Mag City on the screens.

These off-hours gatherings are the hardest for me. I never found it easy to socialize, preferring to stick with Ulna and River rather than be friends with a lot of people. It's difficult for me to open up with strangers. Even though we aren't supposed to be strangers; we are the new Purple Bloods. We are on the same side, and we're supposed to have each other's backs in the Hunt.

They seem so strange to me, these Sixteens from the other communities. They train and talk as if they relish the idea of killing Blue Bloods. How do they put aside their past friendships and relationships so easily and look forward to destroying their opponents in the field? Even if River hadn't entered the Lottery, I would find it hard to want to kill another kid, even for a future filled with wealth and position in Mag City.

Still, as little as I am able to bond with my new peers, I stick close to them, even though I'm on the fringes. I am just avoiding River, I admit it. As this first week unrolls, I find it fairly easy to avoid being alone with him. I know he wants to talk with me privately, but I manage to keep apart from him. What would I say to him, after all? I appreciate you making sure I was safe?

It's written on his face, in his eyes, every time our paths cross in the barracks or in the training rooms. He wants to explain to me why he's come here, to Mag City, why he entered the Lottery. It's just like him, to think he can rescue me somehow from a fate that is written in my blood. He is in love with me, I have to recognize it.

But his feelings are so misguided.

I don't love him. Even if I did, we could never be together, with him being a Blue Blood and me a Purple.

His feelings for me are going to get him killed.

And I will be responsible for his death.

Chapter Six

ON OUR FIFTH OR sixth day of training, Sergeant Krim pulls me aside as we run from the gymnasium back to the barracks for lunch. "Follow me, Recruit," he orders, veering away from the column of Purple and Blue Sixteens. I follow behind, wiping the sweat from my forehead with the sleeve of my practice shirt.

The sergeant leads the way to a cement bench in a park-like area of the military grounds, where flowering trees shade the grassy area from the sun, already high in the sky. There are a number of men and women working throughout the area. By the color of their maintenance uniforms, they must be Blues, trimming hedges and pulling weeds in the flower borders. I wonder if any of them are recent losers in the lottery, who were sitting across from me in the stadium during the drawing.

"I wanted to speak with you about your friend, River," Sergeant Krim says, taking a seat on the bench and gesturing for me to join him. "You've been avoiding him in practice sessions."

"No...not avoiding—"

"Yes, avoiding. You have feelings for him. Maybe he was a friend back home in Eie," Krim says. "That won't serve you well when we enter the Hunt. You need to realize that whatever feelings you have—had—for him, ended when you tested Purple. If one cell in your body somehow believes that you can help him, can save him, then you forfeit your own life. And I won't have it. My recruits don't die. My recruits win."

Looking up at him, a full head taller than me with a strongly-muscled frame, a shiver runs through my body. It must be from the cold cement bench, shaded from the warmth of the sun.

It is impossible that I am feeling anything for him, other than respect and a little fear. He has the power to make my life here hellish, as he has other recruits who have displeased him.

"In case you don't understand me completely, Recruit," he goes on, "I will spell it out for you. You will engage River and every other Blue Blood Lottery winner, every day, and train to the best of your ability. You will not go easy on him or anyone else. You will fight to the death in every exercise, every practice match. And when you reach the Hunt, you will use every advantage you have gained by training with your enemies and learning both their strengths and weaknesses to defeat them."

Then, in absolute defiance of every rule of military discipline I've been learning, Sergeant Krim reaches out to capture my chin in his hand, turning my face upwards toward his. He is touching me, in an intimate way forbidden by military protocol. His dark eyes burn into mine, his lips set in a grim line.

"You. Will. Win."

With that, he releases me, then stands and stalks away across the well-tended grass, leaving me shivering on the bench.

"Again!" The corporal in charge of *Joong bong* staff training drops into a crouching stance in front of me. She moves in swiftly to engage, and my staff smashes into hers with a crash that sends pain flashing through my arm. The strike has cracked open the thin flesh across my knuckles, but I can't spare the time to look down at my injury.

We continue to strike, back, forth, darting in and out with weapons flying through the air with deadly force. I drop to my knees, spinning in under her guard and landing a blow on her torso. She jerks, steps back, out of reach, and I leap to my feet with the staff held defensively in front of me.

The corporal doesn't attack again. Instead, she steps back, a look of shock on her face. Throughout the huge open space of the gymnasium, the sounds of fighting continue, but here, in this one corner of the expansive room, the silence is complete.

“What’s the holdup, Corporal Zynn?” Sergeant Krim stalks across the floor from the other side of the gym, his own staff balanced across his shoulder. The corporal points her staff at my hand, and we all look down. Blood is flowing freely from the crack across my knuckles, running in a zagged streak down the back of my hand and along the curve of my wrist, disappearing beneath the cuff of my sleeve.

“Wha—?” The corporal chokes on the single word.

“Corporal Zynn, stand down,” Sergeant Krim orders. The corporal is still staring at my hand, shock etched upon her face. “Corporal! Stand down!”

She finally moves, lowering her staff to rest one end on the floor at her feet. “Yes...yes, sir!”

Sergeant Krim whips off his black headband, unrolling the fabric quickly and wrapping it over my wound. I am still frozen in place, panting heavily, staring at the impossible sight. The impossible blood color peeking out from beneath the black fabric.

The sergeant grabs my staff and tosses it to Corporal Zynn, who catches it reflexively. Shaking her head, she focuses on the sergeant. “Sarge,” she says slowly, forcing the words out. “Is that —”

“It’s nothing, Corporal,” Sergeant Krim says to her. “Corporal Zynn, return to your barracks. Wait for my orders. Speak to no one. Is that understood?”

“Yes...yes, sir!” Her spine straightens and she whips around, marching over to the staff's rack and putting both our weapons back in their places. I notice, however, that she takes the time to very carefully wipe both staffs down with a cloth, removing any trace of my blood.

“Recruit Kairyn, follow me,” the sergeant orders, once again leading me off to a private area. This is getting to be a habit, it seems. I feel all eyes in the gymnasium following us as we cross the mats to a side door, leading back to the offices and treatment rooms.

How much did they see? I wonder. What did they see? What did *I* just see? I hold the black headband tightly over my bleeding knuckles as I scurry after my commanding officer.

Sergeant Krim strides briskly in front of me, his long steps eating up the length of the interminable corridors. He leads me back through a maze of corridors to an area I haven’t seen yet, in the week I’ve been here. He leads me into an unused office with a bare desk and two chairs. Circling the metal desk, he pulls open a drawer and grabs a first-aid kit, then lifts the second chair over the desk and plants it on the floor beside the first.

"Sit," he orders, not looking me in the face. He's not the kind of officer to avoid confrontation. When he takes my injured hand in his, I can feel a tremor in his broad fingers. Or is it me that's shaking?

Maybe it's both of us.

Sergeant Krim grabs a paper-wrapped gauze pad from the first aid kit and rips it open, spreading the sterile material on top of the desk. Peeling back the black fabric of the headband, he lays my hand atop the gauze. I swallow hard, but my mouth is so dry.

I wish there'd been time to grab a bottle of water from the cooler before we left the gymnasium. I could really use it now.

My hand lies palm down and fingers spread wide on the desk as Krim pulls out a squeeze bottle of disinfectant and more gauze. I can't take my eyes off it, like a dead thing found on the road, run over by a cart.

"If you're going to faint, let me know so I can catch you," Krim says. I don't know if he's joking or not. "The floors in here are solid concrete. We'll have an even bigger mess to deal with if you crack your head open."

So, not joking.

And this truly is no joke.

"How—" I try to articulate my thoughts, but it's not working. "How can...this...*be*?"

The blood spreading across the white gauze pad is not the red I'm used to seeing, when I would fall on the playground and scrape my knee or cut my fingers chopping carrots for dinner. It's not supposed to be red anymore, not since the Testing. No problem. That's normal.

And it's not Blue, but I didn't Test Blue. Expected.

In an effort to regain my grip on reality, I'm checking off the boxes one by one.

My blood—since the Testing, since I received the serum which determined the course of the rest of my life—is supposed to be Purple. I am a Purple.

I am a Purple Blood.

Oma told me so.

The doctor in the Testing tent told me so.

Then how is this even possible?

My blood, staining the gauze soaked with disinfectant as Sergeant Krim wipes my wound clean, is three distinct colors, all suspended in a clear matrix. Purple. Blue. Red. All together. All in me.

In a rush, I lean away from the desk and spew vomit all over the floor and wall, the bitter acid burning my throat. I heave and heave until there's nothing left inside me. My face is wet but not from the vomit. When I reach up with my undamaged hand to wipe my cheeks it comes away wet with tears. They flowed unnoticed, silently. Until now.

Sergeant Krim finishes bandaging my knuckles tightly and pulls me to his chest where I collapse against his shirt, sobbing loudly. He holds me for a long, long time.

When at last I pull away, my flood of tears has left his shirt soaked through. He doesn't seem to mind. He doesn't seem like my C.O. now, either. He seems like a friend.

"Stay here, okay?" Krim says and leaves the room for a minute or two. When he returns, he hands me a bottle of ice-cold water, twisting off the cap for me so I can drink. He opens a second bottle for himself and takes a long swig. Then he takes a third and holds it to my forehead, the coolness relieving the fever I'm feeling.

"Now then," he goes on, "I think we need to talk, you and I."

I give a harsh little laugh. "Ya think?"

He smiles, regret and chagrin mixing in his expression. “There’s something you don’t know about your family.”

“Oma—my mother—told me that I was adopted,” I say quickly. “That’s why I Tested...”

Purple. She told me that’s why I Tested Purple. But I’m not a Purple Blood, am I?

“I know what you were told,” Sergeant Krim says. “I received a message from her immediately after your testing. Your Oma was a friend of my father’s, from way back. He was the one who took you to Eie as an infant and gave you to her to care for. She promised to keep your secret, to protect you, to let you have a normal childhood.” He pauses, shaking his head. “I remember seeing you that night, when my dad brought you to our house, on the way out of the city. I was about two or three years old. I don’t remember much, but my mother told me stories of how a girl will come along someday and change the world.”

“But why couldn’t I stay—”

Why couldn’t I stay with my own mother, here in Mag City? I know why.

I take another long sip of the water, gathering my thoughts. Looking down at my now-bandaged hand, I know exactly why my birth mother couldn’t keep me.

There is a rare exception to the Blood Laws here in Elleon. Everyone is Tested at the age of Sixteen to determine what color the serum we all are given turns our blood. Purple Bloods run our country, fill all the government posts, make all the laws. Purples live in luxury, earned through their efforts to protect the rest of our people. Blue Bloods work to support the rest of the population, including the Purples who rank above them in the social hierarchy.

But above them all, both Purples and Blues, is the ruling family. The rulers of Elleon have blood which contains all three colors, Red, Blue, and Purple. *Lorem Sanguis.* This is a gift from the gods, to make it simple to determine who rules the country.

King Ilan and Queen Helena had a baby Sixteen years ago, the Crown Prince Hern. Hern will rule Elleon when his father is gone. There can be no disputing that fact.

Yet here I am.

Sixteen years old, like Crown Prince Hern, and bearing the *Lorem Sanguis*, the blood of the rulers.

We must have been twins, Hern and me. But I was a girl. By our laws, I would have been put to death, so that I was no threat to Hern's eventual assumption of the throne. Sergeant Krim's father spirited me away, took me to Eie, where Oma raised me as her own.

As soon as anyone saw my blood, they would know who I truly was.

And my life would be forfeit.

Chapter Seven

SERGEANT KRIM REASSIGNS CORPORAL Zynn to a remote border post. He assures me that she won't talk about what she saw. When I see her boarding a transport, she is wearing the stripes of a sergeant, equal in rank to his own. She spots me standing on the grass, just returned from a run, and nods at me. No more than that. But the look in her eyes tells me that she won't reveal my secret.

Thank the gods for that!

It's not just me whose life would be forfeit, even now. Oma. Sergeant Krim. His entire family, even though his father died years ago. Maybe even all of Eie, for harboring me.

It seems like I am living not with royal blood running through my veins, but with solid ice. There is a constant chill I can't overcome, even though I drink hot beverages and layer on extra clothing.

My training can't change, lest it raise suspicions among the other recruits. For the same reason, I can't be given special privileges, like a private room or easier training schedules. Yet, I must be ever-vigilant not to reveal to anyone else the quality of my blood. If the other recruits discovered my secret, well, it wouldn't be a secret for very long.

Before that day in the gymnasium, my life promised to be one of privilege and luxury once I survived the Transcendent Hunt and earned my way into society. Now, I wonder where I will fit in. I must never reveal who I am. I can never let anyone see me bleed. That means never allowing anyone to get close enough to me to be a threat.

I can never fall in love, or get married, or have children of my own. Too much risk of being found out. Even if I am constantly on guard, though, constantly vigilant and careful of every move, how long will I live?

Someone is bound to find out who I am—*what* I am—sooner or later.

For now, all I can do is be extra cautious with every move I make, hyper-aware of my surroundings, so that I never fall or hurt myself in any way. I start wearing extra layers of clothing whenever possible, not just for warmth, but to protect myself from injury. I always choose long sleeves now, and even gloves to protect my hands from further damage.

Plus, the sergeant is watching me like a hawk, ready to swoop in and pluck me away if anything goes wrong.

Suddenly, the unisex shower situation begins to seem threatening. Even with no open wounds to reveal the color of my blood, I begin getting up in the middle of the night to shower when everyone else is asleep.

It's about the middle of the second week—although it's near impossible to tell one day from another here—when we are loaded into a couple of long transport buses and driven outside the city to a fenced-off area on the edge of a wasteland. I've heard about places like this, where the reclamation of ruined land has ceased for lack of funding, or lack of interest. For many decades after the war which gave rise to our great country of Elleon, criminals and prisoners of war were confined in camps and forced to do the work of reclaiming salvageable land ruined in the bombing. I guess this place wasn't worth bothering with.

Sergeant Krim and a trio of lower-level support personnel—each carrying a hefty duffle bag—lead the way as we file out of the buses and take up ranks facing the weathered wooden barricade fence which runs for what seems like miles in either direction. There are viewing platforms spaced out every few hundred yards along the top of the fence, with a catwalk connecting them.

"Recruits, we have a new training exercise for you today," Sergeant Krim's voice carries easily through the still air of early morning. "Based on an ancient military technique known as *parkour de combatant*, or just *parkour*, this exercise will measure your fitness, speed, and agility, as well as your daring and ingenuity."

He gestures for one of the corporals to hand over his duffle bag, which Krim kneels and places on the dirt. Unzipping the top, he pulls out a harness, fitted with some sort of electronic gadgets along the straps. The corporal steps forward and takes it from the sergeant, slipping it over his own chest and snapping it into place at the shoulders and waist.

The other two staffers, another Corporal and a private, move to open the stockade-type gates in the wooden barricade. As the wide barriers open, the ruined town inside is exposed. Narrow streets are filled with wrecked vehicles. Crumbling buildings with blown-out windows line the streets, with doors hanging open or missing completely. There are many piles of rubble where buildings used to stand as well, some chest-high and others towering well above the landscape.

"Recruits," Sergeant Krim calls out again. "Take up a position on the catwalk, half of you on either side." The staffers point out the ladders leaning against the inside of the barricade, and we quickly line up to climb to the top. When it's my turn, I realize that my extra caution is holding up the line. But what choice do I have? If I fall and start bleeding, or even get a splinter through my cloth gloves that makes my hand bleed...

I climb as quickly as I can without injuring myself.

There's an old wooden railing running along the inner edge of the catwalk, which I hold onto with my gloved hands. Twenty feet above the ground, I can't risk a fall, although the other

Purples—the fearless, eager ones—look askance at me. They believe I've lost my nerve, when at first, I was also fearless.

There's nothing I can do to change their impression of me now.

Let them think I'm a coward if they want. It's better to be called a coward than to be executed for my bloodline.

"Corporal Aleci will now demonstrate *parkour de combatant*, running the course while you watch." Below us on the ground, Sergeant Krim waves the man forward, where he takes up a position behind a bright purple line painted on the cracked pavement of the ruined town. "The harness he wears records each move he makes, the effort it takes, and the skill with which he executes it. If he fails a move, slips, or falls the harness records it. If he adds in extra moves, increasing his difficulty, it records that, too. If you look ahead at the course," Krim gestures along the street, where bright purple arrows are painted on every surface, "you'll see these arrows pointing in the direction you should take. The more arrows you include in your run, the more points you score. If you skip arrows, your score diminishes. The object of the course is to get the highest score possible. Corporal Aleci will now demonstrate how to run the course."

The sergeant steps to one side, pulling a whistle from his pocket. He gives one short blast on the instrument and the corporal takes off.

From high above the ground on the catwalk, we watch the corporal race from one obstacle to the next, flinging himself over crumbling walls, swinging from metal poles, jumping over huge holes in the ground in front of him. He darts from one side of the street to the other and back again, never slowing for an instant, a bright light flashing from the back of his harness each time he completes a move. My mouth drops open when he races up a pile of broken cinder blocks, leaps to catch a metal pole with his bare hands, swings his body in a wide circle and then launches himself into the air where he lands on the edge of a roof. He races over the roof as if he's dancing and disappears over the far side, only to reappear farther up the street, leaping from roof to roof of a line of rusted-out vehicles. When he finally reaches the end of the course, he gives a final giant leap into the air, slamming his palm against a purple circle painted on a wall at the end of the street.

A loud buzzer sounds as Corporal Aleci drops to the ground, bent over with his hands braced on his knees as he obviously fights for breath. I am breathing hard myself after just watching his performance. And we are supposed to run this same course.

I glance down at the ground below the barricade fence then, meeting Sergeant Krim's eyes. He's looking directly at me. I swallow, nerves tingling. Am I supposed to do that?

And not injure myself?

The sergeant seems to have an uncanny knack for reading my thoughts. He nods very slightly, enough for me to see, but not so much that anyone else would notice. He's telling me that I can do this. That I *will* do this.

I shudder. I won't let him down, but the fear is real.

For the rest of the day, we are ordered to break up into small groups and practice the moves we saw demonstrated earlier. There are arrows painted throughout the ruined town, on street after street of crumbling buildings and broken pavement, tilted light poles and gaping holes which drop into gaping basements where houses used to stand.

Since we've been here eleven days now - or is it twelve? - I've started to get to know some of the faces around me. Cielo, a light-skinned Blue Blood boy from Eos, joins my group. Ree, a Blue Blooded girl with ebony skin and curly black hair, is also from Eos. And Jeaol, a Purple Blooded boy with golden skin and freckles from Elm that I met on my first day here.

The last person to join the team is River.

His face is solemn when he slides in beside me. "Mind if I join you?" he asks softly.

Cielo steps forward, extending his hand. "Glad to have you, mate!" The boy from Eos turns to grin at us. "River should be great at this," he says. "He told me he grew up climbing trees, so this should be second nature for him."

"He'll be the one to beat," I glance over at River and smile. "We raced up trees in Eie, and he always seemed to win."

I remember climbing trees with River, along the banks of the creek that flowed behind our farmsteads. I also remember skinning my knees on the rough bark, and River plastering mud on to stop the bleeding so we could stay outside until it was too dark to see. Only now if I begin to bleed...

Looking back toward the stockade gates in the barricade fence, I can see Sergeant Krim demonstrating a two-footed jump from high- to mid- to low-level block walls. If I begin to bleed and my group sees the color of my blood, what would Krim do? He sent Corporal Zynn away to some remote outpost to prevent her from spilling my secret. But what would he do to other recruits?

I realize that I know next to nothing about the man. He seems to feel some responsibility for my safety, due to his father having been the one to save me as an infant. He seems to want to keep me from being discovered. To what lengths would he go, really?

Would he kill someone who found me out and threatened to tell?

I want to trust him.

But can I? Really?

My moves throughout the training session are tentative at best. While the others fling themselves from ground to vehicle top to lamp post, I follow cautiously, always weighing the movements before taking the leap.

And while the others seem to be bonding, joking and pushing each other to go higher, faster, to be more daring, I am out on the fringes of the group, following behind. If not for River, hanging back and offering reassurance, I wouldn't be missed if I fell into one of the deep, dark basement craters.

"Ryn, my Grandma could race faster than this," River says with a big grin. "I know you

can do this."

When Krim calls a break for lunch, which the staffers hand out to us in brown paper sacks, I find a spot away from the others, sitting with my back against a wall covered with random splotches of paint.

"You've been avoiding me, Ryn," River says, launching himself over the wall and landing on his heels beside me. He sinks down, opening his lunch sack and pulling out a sandwich. "I came here to make sure you were okay, and for nearly two weeks, I haven't been able to get close enough to say, 'Boo!'"

I knew this moment was coming. I'm actually surprised I've been able to put it off for so long.

"I know," I say. "It's just...now...here."

"Now I'm the enemy," he says softly. "You know I'll never be your enemy, don't you? Ryn, I—"

I throw up my hand, covering his lips. "Don't. Just...don't. It can't happen. Not now. It won't happen."

"I know that," he says. "That doesn't mean I don't still care about you. It doesn't mean I don't care if you're happy, safe, and protected."

"That's not your job, River. Protecting me. It never was."

"I know. I didn't mean it that way," he says, his voice dropping nearly to a whisper. "But I'm your friend, even now. I want to know you're going to be okay. And if entering the Lottery was the only way to be sure of that...Well, I didn't really have a choice, did I?"

Boys can be so stupid sometimes. Sweet, but still stupid.

“You’re not helping me,” I say, shaking my head in exasperation. “You’re going to get yourself killed. And now I have to worry about you every minute. That’s not helping me any, now is it?”

“Well, it’s obvious you need someone to watch out for you!” His voice is raising, but luckily not high enough for anyone to overhear. “What’s with you, Ryn? I’ve never known you to be so...so fearful. You’ve been acting like you’re afraid to pick up a staff or leap a wall. You’ve always been the first one to shimmy up a tree or leap off the cliff into the waterfall.”

I don’t answer. I can’t answer. What could I possibly say to get him to back off?

“Is everything all right here?”

We both turn guiltily to find that Sergeant Krim has snuck up behind the crumbled wall and is leaning over the top, staring down at us. Well, he did want me to change my attitude toward River, to stop running away from him. I don’t think this is what he had in mind, though.

The sergeant wanted me to face River head on, to fight him and win.

He didn’t want me to come close to having a lover’s quarrel. Even though we’re not even lovers.

"Everything's fine," I say, standing up. "We were just discussing the course, and how to do our very best. Right, River?"

"Yeah," he says, gathering up the remains of his lunch and cramming the trash into his bag. "Everything's fine. Strategy. That's what we were talking about."

Krim doesn't look convinced, but he turns and heads back to where the other recruits are sitting just inside the stockade gates. "Finish up people," he orders. "This afternoon you will each run the defined course three times. Your scores will be averaged and recorded. We'll see who has the best score at the end. That recruit will get to sleep in tomorrow and skip the first training session of the day."

Now, that's a prize worth battling for.

As the afternoon wears on, I realize the Blues are watching the Purples as much as we're watching them, trying to suss out the competition, to determine strengths and weaknesses as Sergeant Krim instructed us to. Although the Blue Bloods are supposed to be less than the Purples, I don't think they know it. They will be fighting for their lives, why wouldn't they put more effort into trying to be the best they can be?

By the time the sun is beginning to lower in the sky, the final recruit has run his third course. Sergeant Krim and his staffers huddle around an electronic pad, scrolling through the rankings.

Finally, they turn and head for us where we've all found places to sit or lie on the pavement.

Everyone is exhausted. I know I am. My last course run was absolutely brutal.

"Okay, everybody, listen up!" Corporal Aleci steps forward. "We are delighted—and pretty much shocked—to find we have a tie. Two of you reached the same high score. One Blue and one Purple. Emvy and Jeaol, step forward."

Jeaol is the Purple boy from my practice group, but I've never talked to Emvy, a girl with lightly tanned skin and black hair.

"Both of you have tomorrow morning off from training," the sergeant says. "Enjoy your sleep. The rest of you better start practicing," he goes on. "It's only going to get tougher from here on out. Now, back to the buses."

I trail behind the others, ending up at the back of the line. I glance back at a touch on my arm. River. "We need to talk," he says. I was hoping to avoid this.

He seems to have my best interests at heart. But we've never been more than friends, in my eyes, anyway. Now, when I suspect he wants more from me, wants something he can never have, does that change how he feels? For now, I'll give him the benefit of the doubt.

“Okay,” I agree.

My life is so complicated now, I feel like I’ll never find a safe place to just be me.

And River’s feelings for me have increased those complications by a thousand percent.

Chapter Eight

RIVER AGREED TO MEET me after dinner in one of the game rooms, and I need to figure out what to do about him. Luckily, the barracks are quiet after our *parkour* training day with most everyone hanging out in the common room. I peek through the door on my way to meet River and find that, despite our training together and living in such close quarters, lines have been drawn. Purple Bloods cluster on one side of the big room and Blues on the other.

Shaking my head, I wonder once again why it has to be this way. Has humanity always been so barbaric, that a simple difference in the color of one's blood makes us enemies? It's a wonder we ever crawled out of our caves.

River is already in the game room when I arrive. We settle into a sofa against one wall, hidden in the shadows in case anyone else is roaming the halls and happens to look through the observation window.

I lay into him immediately. "Why did you enter the Lottery?" I ask, needing to know for sure why he came here. I've never led him on. I don't want to assume the worst, but... "How could you possibly think that was a good idea?"

The look in River's eyes is so intense it borders on fanaticism. "I couldn't believe it when you Tested Purple! I thought we'd always be together, in Eie—"

"You are one of my best friends, River," I cut him off. "You've always been my friend! Why would you think I meant anything more to you than that?" Maybe I'm putting my foot in my mouth, but I have to know. "How long have you been thinking that I was more than a friend? That you—That we—" He's set us up for disaster. "When I Tested Purple, you had a perfect excuse for saying goodbye and getting on with your life."

"You are my life, Ryn! You're all I've ever wanted!"

He's not hearing me. He's so wrapped up in his fantasy of a future together that he can't see I never felt about him like he obviously does about me. I never encouraged him, never played with his feelings. I was always perfectly straightforward.

We were friends, nothing more.

"Look, I care about you — so much. It's just not the way you want me to care about you. I never expected to leave Eie. I never wanted to leave my home behind. But the Lottery was the perfect opportunity for you to find someone who would truly love you beyond friendship. If I ever gave you the idea that we could be something other than friends, I'm sorry. If I seem like I'm frustrated, it's because I am. I'm scared to death that you won't make it out of this," I turn my face away to hide my tears. "River, I love you so much it hurts. You're like a brother to me. Siblings protect each other, but I can't protect both of us. Not here. This feels like Mallen and Liiken all over again."

"Ryn, we're not like them!" River protests strongly, but he's blind to the reality of our situation.

I explode. "How are we not like them?! You Tested Blue and I Tested Purple. You followed me here! Why? Did you think you could turn my blood back to Blue, somehow? You've put both our lives in danger!"

River jumps up from the sofa, pacing back and forth on the gaming area marked out on the wooden floor. "I can't believe you'd say that, Ryn! All of our lives we've been together. I saw you every day, summer and winter. When you left, I couldn't face not having you in my life. I wanted—"

I know what he wanted. But we obviously never wanted the same thing.

"You need to talk to Sergeant Krim, tell him you want to drop out," I tell River. "If we meet in the Hunt, I'll have to kill you. And I can't do that. I won't do that."

"I know!" My words seem to have given him fresh hope. That was definitely not my intention. "We can work together, me watching your back and you watching mine. You're not a bad fighter—"

"No! I can't—" How can he be so obtuse? He refuses to see anything beyond his own desires, beyond his own fantasies. This is getting us nowhere.

I need to change the subject so that he stops focusing on me, on what he thinks we can still be to each other. I need to talk to Sergeant Krim. He might be able to do something about River, send him home or something. But for now, I need to keep River from doing anything even more stupid than entering the Lottery.

"What happened to Ulna?" I may be grasping at straws, but I need to distract River until I can figure out what to do with him. "I heard her yell in the Testing tent, but I never saw her after the test. I never got to say goodbye to her."

River gives a harsh laugh. "None of us did."

"What do you mean?" My mind flashes back to that day, almost two weeks ago now. Everyone in the village was there on Testing day, waiting to witness us Sixteens move up into our proper social order.

Everyone was there, even...

Alura, the Red Blood. And that older woman, the one in the wheelchair. The one whose legs corkscrewed from the corrective serum she'd been given when she Tested Red.

"Did Ulna...Was Ulna...?"

River has turned away, his head drooping. He can't look me in the eyes.

"Ulna Tested Red Blooded, didn't she?" I shudder, thinking of my other friend undergoing the corrective treatment for the worst deformity in our world: Testing Red. "That's why she wasn't outside, in the Blue chairs. Right? They'd taken her away, to give her the corrective serum—"

"Ye-e-es," River says slowly, still hiding his face from me. "She Tested Red. But—"

"But what?!" Horror filled me at the thought of Ulna undergoing the barbaric treatment, imagining the damage it could have caused to her beautiful face, to her slim body. "She...did she... die?"

Not everyone survived the second treatment. Some, like Alura and that older woman, were left with painful, permanent deformities, it was true. But some people who were given the corrective serum were unable to survive the treatment at all, their inner organs so corrupted that they ceased to breathe or pump blood through their twisted, mangled hearts.

"No, Ulna didn't die," River says, and I relax a tiny bit. Too soon. "She didn't die because she didn't take the serum," he goes on.

That was impossible. No Red Blood was allowed to live among us, lest they corrupt the bloodlines. Another example of the barbarism of our social order. All Red Bloods were Treated with the corrective serum, to turn their blood Blue. There was no other option. Except—

"Are you saying that Ulna—"

River turns back abruptly, crossing the few feet between us and dropping to his knees in front of me where I sit on the edge of the sofa. He takes my icy cold hands in his, squeezing gently. In his eyes, I see the truth I've been avoiding ever since he arrived, not wanting to admit that there could be anything so horrifying for me to face.

But his words give me no choice.

"Ulna ran."

While it's true that Elleon has been at peace with our neighbors to the north for over a hundred years, that doesn't quite hold true for the southern borderlands. We aren't actively engaged in a declared conflict with Old Mexico, but those who live along the border have frequently interacted with Elleon's border communities. And those interactions are often tense.

That isn't the real problem, however. The southern borderlands are where our own outcasts hide out. People like Ulna, who Tested Red Blooded, but refused to submit to the corrective treatments.

When I return to the common area after leaving River in the game room, I find a place between the two groups of recruits, hovering between them. Close to my Purple comrades-in-arms, but near enough to the Blues to overhear their conversation. There are a wide range of seating choices: floor pillows are stacked along the walls during the day, and we spread them wherever we want to sit, or curl up on an assortment of sofas and armchairs. I choose an overstuffed chair where my head barely shows above the back, all but unseen. I find it's easier to gather intelligence this way, being in the room but unnoticed.

In our small outer communities, rumors abound. Gossip is the way we entertain ourselves through long days of backbreaking labor. Even kids still in school learn to share tidbits of salacious talk about the Red Rebellion, the greatest threat to Elleon's stability. It's become a standard topic of conversation, the developments along the border.

Even the Purples discuss the Red Rebellion endlessly, since that's where any who choose the military as a career will most likely end up. Fighting Red Bloods who fled their home communities. Those are the ones—like Sergeant Krim—who really maintain our stratified society. They not only train new recruits, but also run the military and maintain the safety and security of Elleon against all threats, foreign and domestic.

And the greatest domestic threat we face is the Red Blood Rebellion.

Everyone has heard the disturbing rumors of Sixteens who Tested Red Blooded, but rather than face lifelong disability after undergoing the correction for their blood anomaly, escaped into the wilds and badlands along the southern border, those parts of the country which remain damaged by the war leading to Elleon's creation after the old world crumbled. There they live in secret enclaves, plotting insurrection.

I am much more highly motivated to gather Red Rebellion intelligence now that I know my other friend has most likely joined the terrorists. And the Blue Bloods don't disappoint, although I wasn't expecting to hear this—

"I've heard the other staff call him Reap," Emvy, the Blue Blooded girl from Elm who tied for the lead in today's *parkour* training, is saying to the boy who sits beside her on a floor pillow. "I'm sure he's the one."

"So, just because you heard someone call Sergeant Krim 'Reap,' you think that he's the infamous Reaper?" the boy's tone is filled with disbelief.

"Think about it," Emvy insists. "He's the right age. He's pretty highly ranked for someone his age, so he has obvious battlefield experience. What if he is the same one?"

"What would The Reaper be doing here in Mag City, training green recruits for the Hunt?" Jae, another boy from Elm, and Emvy's boyfriend, pulls a couple more big floor pillows off the stack in the corner of the room, tossing them down beside Emvy and her companion. He flops down, leaning back with his fingers laced beneath his head and closing his eyes. "Why would they waste someone of his talents here, when he could be squashing those Reds like bloody little bugs?"

I sink lower in my chair, making sure my head doesn't show above the back. No one knows that my friend may even now be making her way south to join the rebels. I'm sure River wouldn't tell anyone but me. But if it's true that Krim has fought—and killed—rebels in the south, what does it mean that he's here, now?

He knew about me. He's here training me. Does he know about Ulna? Does he think that I am somehow a way into the Reds camp, because of my friend?

I was beginning to trust him. But now I feel completely isolated again.

The voices behind me drop, but I still can hear what the Blues are saying.

"My brother entered the Lottery three years ago," Jae is saying. I peek around the side of my chair and see that he's sitting up again, elbows perched on his knees and a scowl on his face. "He wasn't chosen in the Lottery, so we know he didn't die in the Hunt. So, tell me where he is now? Why hasn't he ever written home? If they really do give the losers from the Lottery menial jobs here in Mag City, why do half of them disappear forever? Why doesn't anyone ever hear from them again? I'll tell you why —"

Emvy reaches out and places her finger on his lips. "Shhh! Be careful, Jae," she says. "You never know who's listening."

I close my eyes as if I'm napping, and not a moment too soon. I feel the air currents shift around me as someone—Emvy? Jae?—comes up behind my chair. I don't move. They don't speak. But after long moments pass and I don't hear anything more from behind me, I peek past the side of the chair and see that the small group of gossiping Blue Bloods has moved into a far corner.

I'm learning more every day I'm here, and most of it is stuff I didn't want to know. Life is a lot more complicated here than I ever imagined.

It takes me hours to fall asleep that night. And I don't feel rested at all when the next day finally dawns.

Chapter Nine

THE NEXT DAY'S TRAINING goes badly from the start. Sergeant Krim is in a foul mood, and he pushes us harder than ever. He is an even-handed torturer, I'll give him that. He brutalizes us equally, Purple Bloods and Blue Bloods alike. We start the morning with a twenty-mile forced march outside of the city, then back to the gymnasium for an intense calisthenic workout. We barely have time to gobble down half a lunch before we're ordered out to the buses again for the second day in a row. This time, we end up at a city facility with an enormous indoor swimming pool.

Our training gear doesn't include anything to swim in.

"Line up!" Sergeant Krim orders, and we do, somewhat hesitantly edging up to the rim of the pool. Some of the recruits look absolutely petrified, and I recognize a few of the kids are from desert communities. They obviously haven't grown up swimming and the wide expanse of gently lapping water at their feet terrifies them.

Glancing down the line I find River looking back at me. Unlike some of the others, we grew up swimming in the streams and ponds around Eie. It's second nature for us to be in the water. I give him a sly smirk. We can handle this challenge.

Krim blows a piercing shriek on a metal whistle. "Strip down to your underwear," he orders, and although a few hesitate, we've become accustomed to sharing the barracks' facilities now. Still, no one looks at their fellows as we shrug out of our training uniforms and drop them on the cement floor behind us, along with our boots and socks.

"Now then," the sergeant paces along the floor behind our long line, forty-seven of us Sixteens—seventeen Purple Bloods and thirty Blue Bloods mingled together—beginning to shiver in the coolness of the pool enclosure. "You will encounter water hazards along the Hunt course. You may find yourself needing to wade across creeks, to swim lakes, even to hide among the reeds in a marsh, whatever it takes to escape your pursuers or to hunt down your prey. If you cannot manage in the water, you need to know it now, so that there are no surprises when the Hunt begins."

I am shivering now, from the coolness of the air or from the chill in Krim's voice, I don't know which. Up to now, our training has focused on defense, on survival. Suddenly it's striking a place deep inside me, a place of insecurity and fear, that I might not make it through the Hunt. Each of us is alone in this, fighting for our survival. That's what our entire training has been based upon.

Breaking us down, tearing us apart, so that we don't hesitate to kill each other.

"One blast," the sergeant brings his metal whistle to his lips and gives a short whistle, "and you will jump into the water. There, you will tread water for two hours. Two blasts," he raises his whistle again and gives two sharp tweets on the instrument, "means you may leave the pool. Anyone who leaves the water before the time is up will be punished."

He doesn't say what that punishment will be, but I don't have to worry. I have lived in the water in the summertime since I was three or four years old. I could tread water for days, I'm sure.

Sergeant Krim gives a single blast of his whistle and we're in the water. I swim easily away from the crowd, seeking some space to float alone. But with so many of us in the pool, there are really only a few feet between recruits. I wave my hands through the water with a languid motion, conserving energy as I listen to the splashing of those around me.

I was lucky to have grown up swimming in the streams around Eie, as was River. Some of the other recruits grew up in places without freshwater to swim in and never learned how. They start having trouble almost immediately, sinking below the water after only five or ten minutes.

Sergeant Krim and his corporals stand, arms folded across their chests, watching us implacably. They make no move to help those who are struggling. When a girl near me in the water—I think her name is Nria—goes down for the third time, I swiftly paddle over and reach down to twine my fingers through her long hair, pulling her head back above the water.

"Nria! Try to relax! I've got you."

She is choking, gasping for air and spitting out water. I know that rescuing someone who is drowning is the quickest way to drown yourself, but I can't just watch another kid die when I am such a strong swimmer.

"Relax," I order again, letting go of her hair and wrapping my elbow beneath her chin, forcing her face out of the pool. "Just relax and float. I'll keep your head above water."

Nria struggles *not* to struggle, finally relaxing enough that her legs and belly float up to the surface while I tread water for both of us. I cradle the back of her head against my chest, talking softly, encouragingly, to keep her from panicking again. I see others around me helping those who are weak swimmers. I can't imagine how we're going to last two hours like this, though.

Cielo, the Blue Blooded boy from Eos, is the one who organizes us. "Everyone, help the person next to you!" he calls out. "Pair up. We're not fighting against each other now, we're fighting *for* each other."

Out of the corner of my eye, I see Sergeant Krim stiffen, his usual scowl deepening. In the pool there is no difference between us, no Purple or Blue insignia on a uniform to tell us apart. Now everyone is following our lead, reaching out to help each other stay afloat.

As I look around, I can see that some natural instinct has pulled us into a rough circular formation, facing inwards. Looking around the circle I can see the eyes of my fellow recruits and Lottery winners. There is a mixture of expressions written on the faces of the boys and girls in the big pool. Determination. Exhaustion. Hope. Fear. Confidence. We can all do this if we work together, helping the weaker swimmers.

In return, maybe they'll help those who are weaker at shooting, or running, or whatever. For the first time, I am beginning to glimpse a society where we don't take sides based on our blood.

While I can see that more people are beginning to tire, I know we've been in the pool less than an hour. The corporals standing behind Sergeant Krim are looking nervous. The sergeant's face is stony when he raises his whistle again and gives two sharp blasts.

"Out of the water!"

Too soon.

I have a bad feeling about this.

Like a bunch of waterlogged rats, we swim for the side of the pool, helping the weaker ones reach the cement edge and working with others to heave their quaking bodies up and out of the water. When we're all out, shivering in our sodden underwear on the soaked cement floor, everyone's skin is wrinkled.

I stand beside Nria, a hand on her shoulder for reassurance. She doesn't seem to notice, helpless tears streaming down her face. The emotional toll this sadistic training is taking on the weaker ones among us is really starting to show.

Sergeant Krim stalks along the line of huddled recruits and lottery winners, his face stormy as he looks each of us in the face. Many pairs of eyes drop, unable to meet his gaze. But others—myself among them—stare straight ahead, refusing to back down.

The only sounds in the echoing, high-ceilinged room are waves gently lapping at the side of the pool and teeth chattering as we stand there in our wet underwear, arms wrapped around ourselves for a little warmth. Finally, Krim breaks the silence.

"What. Was. THAT!" He is livid, his face redder than if he'd been standing outside in full sun all day. "Are you really all that stupid? Do you think you can play lifesaver one day, and then go out and Hunt down your prey the next? You are in for the fight of your lives. You will live or die in the Hunt, and you have no choice but to kill or be killed. There is no honor in saving your opponent. There is only death. This is how our society functions. This is the only way for you to ensure that your futures are long and happy ones."

Krim falls silent, turning away. It's as if he's trying to figure out how to punish us for having the audacity to be born. He stands there in silence, and when he turns to face us again, his eyes are no longer angry, just cold. There seems to be something sad about him now, though, and for a moment I feel sorry for him.

If this really is the soldier they call The Reaper, he isn't at all what his reputation says he should be.

I get the definite impression that Sergeant Krim has a heart hidden behind his black uniform.

"Get dressed. Get on the bus. You're all confined to your racks until further notice."

Chapter Ten

AS THE DATE SET for the start of the Transcendent Hunt draws closer, I expect that we will pull further apart, Purples and Blues. But something changed during that hour in the pool when we kept each other afloat. It's a subtle change, but definitely there. By unspoken agreement, we all try to keep it under wraps so Sergeant Krim doesn't get wind of our own small rebellion. At times, though, I wonder how he can't see how we've all changed.

Not all, maybe. But many of us have become more open to our peers. Not our blood peers, but to our fellow Sixteens, the other kids who for one of two reasons thought their lives were about to improve.

Purple Bloods who saw their Testing as a stepping-stone to a life of importance, of wealth and luxury, in Mag City.

Blue Bloods who saw their Lottery win as a way to help their families, while finding a better, easier job here in the capitol of Elleon.

Of just under fifty Sixteens living and training together, thirteen of us Purples and all thirty Blues are working together in training sessions, helping each other to improve their skills. There are only four Purples who can't be trusted to join us. Those who are too self-important, or too violent by their natures, to sacrifice their immediate rewards for the greater good. The rest of us practice together for hours, increasing our fitness and stamina. Most of all, we look out for each other, pulling together as a bulwark against those few who remain dedicated to killing their enemies.

I don't know how, but we are going to get through the Transcendent Hunt together, all of us. Blues and Purples. I try not to even think about the effect this will have when we enter the Hunt grounds.

There are adult Hunters, those chosen in a lottery of their own to win the chance to relive their former glory days when they were Sixteens and came here to Mag City after their own Testing. They will be Hunting all of us, to win prizes and favor. We have been planning ways to defeat them, keep all of us safe.

Worse still, there are members of the Elleon military forces, soldiers chosen from their units to join the Hunt. Highly trained, these men and women will be nearly impossible to defeat. We cannot turn our weapons on them. That would be treason. So, we will have to find other ways to save ourselves from these brutal Hunters.

Soon, there are only three days until the Hunt begins. It will run for twelve hours throughout an abandoned, ruined city to the west. Twelve hours in which we need to protect our fellow Sixteens, our friends. And that protection starts now.

It's three o'clock in the morning and the barracks and training rooms are silent. Not a shadow moves throughout the deserted corridors. Not a shadow, except those cast by our furtive steps. Half of the Blues are heading for the armory, including River, the remainder staying back to cover for their bunkmates. But with those four Purples who haven't joined us sleeping in our bunkroom, only five of us dare to slip out and join the Blues in our carefully planned sabotage.

The armory is a separate building, attached to the rear of the training complex by a short causeway. We slip through the outer causeway doors, plastering ourselves against the walls while Elidys, a girl from the tech community of Mio, hurries up to the inner doors. Elidys had been apprenticed in a manufactory where they made electronic locks. She devised a tool from stolen bits and pieces of tech, and now uses it to unlock the armory door, leading us inside.

The gadget which unlocked the door wasn't Elidys' only creation. In the two weeks since the pool, she's been hard at work every spare minute, figuring out how to sabotage the Purples' weapons. We each carry a tiny handheld device of our own and spread out throughout the darkened room, the only illumination a dim glow from emergency lights set near the ceiling. In the dim room, we set to work.

The weapons provided for the Hunt are massively unequal. Purple Hunters are allowed to carry any number of electronic weapons, including lasers of all sorts which fire bursts of microwaves to disable targets, and light beams which can cut a person in half at 200 yards. Other, more conventional rifles use electronic sighting systems to track down targets and zero in on them, firing bullets which follow targets so they can't escape a killing bullet. Likewise, there are visual and auditory tracking devices, to search out targets so that they can be run down and stabbed with bayonets, swords, or long knives, or shot with small arms.

Using our handheld devices, we spread out among the racks of weapons. Everyone works quickly, in absolute silence, the only sound a tiny beep from our devices each time we hold it next to the electronic control mounted on each weapon and disable the internal controls. When fired, the weapons will appear to be working. But nothing lethal will shoot out of the barrels of the guns. These high-powered rifles will kill no one now.

"Done?" Wadyn, a Purple boy from Mey, slides up beside me. I've been so intent on my task that I didn't notice the others heading for the doors.

I push the button on my device one more time, disabling a high-powered laser rifle, and hear the tiny beep in the otherwise silent room. “Done.”

We head for the others huddling inside the doors.

“Let’s go,” Elidys whispers, pushing open the door into the causeway. We follow her out, racing for the inner doors.

“Mission accomplished, I assume?” As the interior doors open in front of us, we all stop short, piling up on top of each other. Sergeant Krim steps into view. He is in full uniform, but unlike our training sessions, when he is always backed up by his corporals, he is alone. And I know that the rifle resting over his shoulder is not one that we’ve disarmed. “Common room. Now. And keep it quiet.”

One by one we file past him into the long corridor. I am chilled to the bone, as I’m sure everyone else is. In a second, it becomes clear to me that our act of insurrection was anticipated. The sergeant has been watching us all closely lately.

He probably knew what we would do before we figured it out ourselves.

When we reach the lighted common area, we file inside and just stand there. There’s no possible way we can explain what we’ve been doing. No way to turn this into something acceptable. We are traitors, to Elleon and to the crown. Sergeant Krim follows us into the room and stands in the middle of our huddled group of insurrectionists, turning slowly on his heel to take in each and every guilty face.

He stops in front me, but I can't meet his eyes. I have so many conflicting feelings about him. At one time he seemed to be on my side. But there's no way he will forgive my actions tonight. He's probably wishing his father left me to die in the palace, the forbidden twin, and not carried me off to grow up in obscurity in Eie.

Krim reaches out with one finger extended, lifting my chin into the air. When my eyes meet his, I see...

Not hatred.

Not betrayal.

He looks...*proud*.

Finally, he steps away, waving us all in to stand close to him in a huddle. River gets right in front of him, making the first move.

"Is this where you get rid of us, Reaper?"

River's aggression doesn't seem to faze the sergeant.

"This is where," Krim says slowly, "I finally know I can trust you. Yes, I am known as The Reaper, for my activities in the field, eliminating Red Bloods who wanted to wipe out civilized society. I won't deny it. I won't defend it. It was my job." His eyes stray to find me again, standing behind some other kids to his left. "But recently something has reminded me of a promise I made my father, a long time ago. I promised him that I would always choose the honorable path in any conflict. And watching you train," his eyes are focused on mine, and he doesn't look away for a second, "I discovered that what I thought was right, what I'd trained myself to believe was right, is not what Elleon needs. It has become clear to me that we're going down the wrong road, tearing ourselves apart, because of a difference we can't even see. And that needs to change."

It doesn't seem possible. Is it the fact that my blood is *Lorem Sanguis*? Or that I reached out to help a struggling swimmer in the pool? Or has he somehow read my own doubts about what we stand for and discovered that he felt the same way? Whatever it is, it seems I've been wrong about Krim.

He's not my enemy.

"I've been watching you, Recruits," Sergeant Krim says. "Watching you work together, help each other. Watching you devise a plan and plot to overthrow the entire reason for the Hunt. Your sabotage of the weapons stores was a stroke of genius. But you're going to need to do more. *We're* going to need to do more. I've got some plans of my own, based on intel you know nothing about. Will you trust me to help you?"

And so, the sergeant fills us in on the basics of his plan, although he's keeping some of the details to himself. Probably a wise thing to do. There are too many of us to be completely safe. One weak link...

When we finally break up and return to our racks, slipping back into the bunkrooms as the sky is lightening with the first streaks of dawnlight, I finally feel like I have a place in this world. I'm not drifting any longer, unsure what I want from my future.

I finally feel like I have a future. And I'm not going to let it get away.

Chapter Eleven

IN THE LATE AFTERNOON two days before the Hunt, we are taken to a glittering building in the center of Mag City. We are to celebrate at a fancy banquet in the finest hotel in Elleon. Tonight, we'll meet King Ilan and Queen Helena in person before the Hunt. My real parents.

But no one will ever know.

The buses pull up beneath a portico held aloft by carved columns. The glass-fronted building soars forty or fifty stories into the air, reflecting back the golden rays of the lowering sun. Straight-backed men in Blue uniforms usher all of us Recruits inside an enormous lobby filled with white sofas and glass-topped tables.

In an uneven line we straggle across the open space to gilt-railed staircases which rise up on each side. The boys are led up one side and the girls the other. Looking across the open air between the staircases I see the boys being led down a wood-paneled hallway beneath brass chandeliers. Turning back, I find a woman in a Blue uniform matching those worn by the men outside the doors.

“This way, miss,” she says, waving me down the hallway. I see the last of my fellow recruits disappearing through another pair of doors and hurry to follow the woman inside.

We are in a large, high-ceilinged room, filled with tall-cushioned chairs on rotating stands, each placed in front of a vanity table with a huge mirror. On the tables are what look like instruments of torture. A few years ago, one of the traders brought a couple of floppy books filled with photographs of beautiful women in fancy clothes to Eie. Magazines, he called them. Those magazines showed women sitting in chairs just like these while other women fixed their hair and applied makeup to their faces, making them look glamorous.

These instruments of torture are supposed to make us beautiful.

“Ready for your makeover, miss?”

The other girls have already disappeared behind a series of screens into cubicles, the first of them coming back out wearing a pink bathrobe in a silky Mag City fabric. More of the girls come out and are led to chairs in front of the vanity tables before I’ve even stepped inside my own cubicle. An attendant follows me inside.

"Take off your uniform and leave it on the bench," she tells me. "When you're ready, put on the robe and step outside. I'll be prepping you for the banquet." She flings a curtain closed behind me, leaving me alone. I quickly strip out of the gray uniform I've worn since arriving in the city a month ago, slip on the robe, and step outside in my bare feet.

The marble floor is cold on the soles of my feet as the attendant leads me to a chair near the end of the long row. The next hour passes like a dream as every inch of me, it seems, is pampered and primped. My hair is washed in a little rolling sink, then trimmed, curled, and styled like a real Purple Blooded woman. I am manicured and pedicured and made up to look like one of the women in that magazine I saw so long ago, watching the proceedings in the mirror as if I am watching another girl undergoing some strange ritual.

Finally, each of us is led over to the side of the room where we are to be dressed for the banquet.

First, we are given underwear, but unlike anything I've ever seen before. The bras are satiny and lacy, looking like they'd fall apart at the first washing. Totally not your standard-issue military uniform underwear. The panties are even worse: sheer strips of fabric you can see right through, edged in matching lace.

Once I've been given my underwear and led into another cubicle to put it on, the attendant takes my robe and leads me out into the open room. Like the other girls, I glance at my peers but quickly look away. It seems indecent somehow to see my fellow Recruits in such revealing garments. For once, I'm glad that the boys are not sharing our dressing room.

Underwear like we've been given is something I can only imagine a married woman wearing, not a young girl. Not me. But we are not given time to be embarrassed as we are ushered over to be dressed for the fancy party.

There is a row of tall mirrors lining the walls behind huge racks of fancy dresses hanging in a rainbow of colors. These are in even finer fabrics than I've seen on Purples here in Mag City. They look like something the queen herself would wear, long gowns that sweep the floor. The attendants hold up one after the other to my front, standing behind me and looking over my shoulder at my reflection in the mirrors to see how they look. They finally settle on a shimmering sheath in shades of rose, violet, and green, looking like a wash of paint, all the colors running together. The dress has only one long sleeve, the other shoulder left bare. It feels indecent to show so much skin in public, but some of the other girls are in even more revealing gowns.

A pair of silk stockings are rolled up my legs, held up with a lacy item called a garter belt. Then they fit me with a pair of shiny shoes with tall heels, so unlike anything I've ever worn before. All of us teeter around on the strange shoes, trying to find our balance. These are nothing like our boots, or the sturdy shoes I am used to wearing back in Eie. I'm glad these are not a part of our uniforms. I could never escape an enemy running in such treacherous footwear.

When I'm dressed and coiffed to the attendants' satisfaction, I join the other Sixteens near the outer doors on a delicate gilt-painted chair. I turn to the girls next to me, Emvy and Radyn, and smile tentatively.

"I'm so nervous!" Radyn says, holding out her hand to show us how badly she's shaking.

"Me, too!" Emvy whispers.

We are so much alike, even with our differences in blood. One Purple. One Blue. And me. But we all grew up in a provincial community, far from the wealth and luxury of the capitol. It is only an accident of genetics which led us here, or the luck of the draw in the Lottery.

When the doors open to reveal the boys standing in the hallway outside, along with Sergeant Krim, I am anxious to get this evening over with. But it seems we're to have a final lecture before we join the Mag City Purples at the banquet.

"This is a very important night for you all," the sergeant says, his face set in its usual stern lines. "You may think this is a party to celebrate your participation in the Transcendent Hunt. That is only partially true." He pauses, looking around at his Recruits, weighing us and our prospects. "The people you will meet tonight are not here to encourage you in the Hunt. They're here to observe, to weigh your prospects, to try to ferret out your weaknesses. Be friendly, be pleasant, but give nothing away, about your training or—"

His words cut off, but forty-three of us know what he's referring to.

The Plan.

"Be especially careful with the champagne," Krim goes on. "Most of you have never drunk alcohol before, and if you have, it's been provincial beer or mead. The champagne will go to your head without you even noticing, and you won't be able to function tomorrow."

Tomorrow is the last day before the Hunt. In the morning, we return to the stadium for a public exhibition of our new-learned skills. Many—if not all—of the adult Purples at tonight's banquet will be in the stands tomorrow, watching our performance.

Trying to figure out which of us are the most dangerous, the most likely to succeed or fail. They want to see which of us new Purples are worth the time that's been spent training us.

And—no doubt—they want to see if The Reaper has lived up to his reputation, passing on his skills as a killer.

Sergeant Krim isn't done with his warnings yet. "A Recruit with a hangover is a dead Recruit. Watch out for those who try to get you to match them drink for drink. It's a cruel game they play every year. Don't fall for it. Don't let them pressure you into drinking too much. I'll be watching to make sure you don't forget that. Your lives depend on it."

With that, Sergeant Krim leads us back down the hallway to the glittering lobby. We stop at the top of the sweeping stairway. Music plays below from a trio of musicians perched on a small stage which has been set up to one side. Looking down, we get our first glimpse of the Purple Blooded guests filling the lobby to watch us enter the banquet. The number of implacable faces turned upwards to stare at us in our finery is frightening; so many strangers in one place.

Many of these people want to weigh their prospects, to choose their victims in the Hunt.

Little do they know that the game is about to change.

None of us will fall to them. But is the reverse also true?

Chapter Twelve

SERGEANT KRIM WAS RIGHT. Wait staff circulate constantly with trays of filled champagne glasses, the slender flutes looking tremendously refreshing with little beads of perspiration running down their sides. "Take one glass and hold on to it," he says as we descend the staircase as a group and enter the party. "Raise it to your lips, but don't drink. Make it last the evening."

The champagne flute in my hand is rapidly warming in the crowded room. I followed the flow of guests from the lobby into the banquet room, a noncommittal smile plastered on my lips. One well-dressed person after the next comes up to introduce themselves, until the names and faces blur into meaninglessness. The room is too warm and too crowded, the talk too loud. Everything is glitter and light, beautiful women and men dressed in amazing clothes, a swirl of color.

Yet, for all the glamour, these Purple Blooded adults seem like a pack of wolves circling their prey.

After a half an hour of intense scrutiny, it seems like some of us have been shunted aside. I join a couple of the other Recruits,

Wadyn and his twin sister Radyn, at the serving tables at the rear of the high-ceilinged room. It's quieter here, a relief after the crush in the rest of the party.

"So, are we allowed—" I wave my hand over the long, white-draped tables loaded down with enormous trays of food. I've never seen such a feast in my life. There's a pile of china plates at one end, but I don't know what the protocol is for eating at an event like this.

A Blue uniformed man leans over the table, one of the rank of servers lined up behind the huge array of delicacies. "You'll need to wait until after the Royals arrive, Miss," he says in a low voice. "But if you were to sneak a bit, we won't tell anyone."

The other servers nearby smile secretively, as if we're all in on a conspiracy. Wadyn grabs a small roll stuffed with meat and cheese, while Radyn takes a bit of pastry rolled around a vegetable filling. I pluck a strawberry from a luscious looking pile of fresh fruit, then another.

I turn my attention back to the partygoers circulating beneath the crystal chandeliers. There are distinctive clusters here and there, two or three of the Lottery winners in the center of a circle of smiling Purple adults who are shooting questions at them, one after the other. In contrast, the new Purple Recruits are definitely being neglected.

“I wonder how they know?” I say quietly as Radyn reaches back for another tiny pastry.

“Know what?” she asks.

“Which ones of us are Purples and which are Blue. It’s not like we’re wearing badges that identify us by Blood color. Don’t you see it?”

Radyn nods, looking aside at her brother. “We noticed. They’re zeroing in on the Blues, trying to suss them out. They’re like a school of sharks, circling an injured seal.”

“A what?” I have no idea what she’s talking about.

Wadyn laughs harshly. “She’s a Drylander, Raddie,” he says. “Our community, Mey, is on the ocean. A shark is a large predator that hunts in a pack, and a seal is a furry animal. The shark’s preferred prey.”

“Okay,” I say. “But how do they know what our Blood color is? They’re not ‘circling’ us.”

Wadyn and Radyn both Tested Purple. The brother reaches around to pull a slender brochure from beneath his suit jacket where he’s had it tucked into the waistband of his pants. He hands it to me and a chill shivers through my body.

In cheery writing across the top, the brochure says, *Meet Your Prey!* Beneath the writing is a photo of the Blue Lottery winners standing beneath the names of their home communities on the stadium field, that first day in Mag City. I open the cover and flip through the brochure.

Each page features the photos of three Lottery winners with the name of their community printed at the top. Beside each photo is personal information: name, strengths, weaknesses. Is a Blue good at hand-to-hand fighting, but scored poorly at target shooting? That information is there, in black and white.

Times on the parkour course.

Natural swimmer, or never swam before.

Skill with knives and clubs and staves.

Everything they need to know to judge their opponents' skills is right here on paper. I flip to the back, where it lists all of the new Purple recruits. There isn't as much info on us as there is on the Blues.

"Where did you get this?" I ask Wadyn.

He gestures with his champagne glass, now less than half-full. "Over there," he says, pointing toward a table in one corner. I see a couple of Blue Blood Lottery winners wandering in that direction, but two men in military uniforms take up a position in front of the purple-draped table, sending them back into the crowd.

Behind the officers, there is a cluster of women, heads together over one of those brochures. They flip through the pages, laughing at one photo or another and then pointing to one of our Blues.

They're evaluating their prey.

Which of these glamorous women will be on the Hunt in two days' time, trying to kill us?

More than ever, I am convinced of the rightness of our plan. Of our insurrection.

By the time King Ilan and Queen Helena arrive at the banquet and take their seats on the dais, my hunger has passed. When the crowds begin thronging to the serving tables, I hang back. My flute of champagne is empty and I'm thirsty, but I've taken Sergeant Krim's words to heart.

No more alcohol.

"Can you—" I hold my empty glass out to one of the circling servers and she takes it with a smile.

"Would you like another?"

I shake my head. "No. No more alcohol."

She leans in closer, so that no one can hear her words. "I can bring something else, non-alcoholic. No one will know the difference."

I smile gratefully, and within seconds she's back with another glass, the liquid inside still bubbly like champagne, but slightly lighter in color. "We try to watch out for you kids," she says. "You've got a real challenge ahead of you."

I get the impression she thinks I'm a Blue Blood. She must not have seen the photos in that brochure. I don't correct her impression. But as I look around at my fellow Recruits, I see that slightly lighter shade of liquid in many of the glasses they hold.

There's an element of the Blue Blood underclass here in Mag City that watches out for their own, in some small way. Good to know.

I continue to circle, my facial muscles stiff now and beginning to ache from the tension of smiling. My feet are starting to hurt, too, from the high heels. And while the room is too warm, my naked arm and shoulder seem frozen. Eventually, my circling takes me through a series of small tables where people stand with their fully-laden plates of food, gobbling down delicacies. On the far side, there is a row of live trees in huge pots, perfect cover.

I perch on the rolled edge of one of the pots, a hanging branch brushing my bare shoulder. If I thought I could get them back on, I would take off my shoes, just for a few minutes relief. But I can't risk it, not at a fancy party like this. If anyone found me barefoot, they'd think I was just another barbarian from an outer community, unfit for society.

Sighing, I toss back the glass of not-champagne, feeling a little belch rising.

"I thought I saw you disappearing," Sergeant Krim says, materializing around the end of the row of trees.

I swallow back my belch quickly. "I just needed a little break."

"It's hard, I know," he says. "I remember my Hunt Banquet. There were no fewer than three women who wanted to meet me after the Hunt. If I survived, that was." He sips from a glass of his own. The liquid is a lighter color. "I didn't take them up on their offers."

"So you didn't find Mrs. Right," I say with a sly grin. "Pity." Krim rolls his eyes. "Purple women are... well, just look around."

I need to change the subject before I say something that I can't take back.

"Did you know about the brochures they're handing out?"

He looks somewhat abashed. "I did. I thought you all had enough to deal with. You didn't need any further proof of how barbaric this entire set-up is, so I didn't share that bit of intel with you." He turns and captures my chin in his fingers. I can feel the calluses on his fingertips scratch my skin. "I don't want you to worry, Kairyn. Our plan will work."

I pull back from his too-intimate touch. "Why?"

"Why what?" he asks.

"Why now? Why are you willing to risk your entire career to help us?"

He grimaces. "I've been in charge of Transcendent Hunt training for two years now. When I discovered that you were among the Recruits this year, well...I've hated this system all my life, since I was old enough to understand what it all meant. You, Kai...you are something special, something that's never been seen here in Elleon before. People will fight with you. Fight for you. To change this whole sick system. There have been signs for years now that we are failing, that our entire society is built on quicksand. You are a symbol of what could be."

I snort, holding up my empty glass and peering through the thin crystal. Maybe I should have gone with the real champagne after all.

"No pressure or anything, right?"

Krim smiles, taking the empty flute from my fingers. "Do the impossible. No pressure"

I can't hold back the champagne belch any longer, letting it rip. *Blrrrt!* I grin, a perfect example of a savior. "Sure! Why not?"

Chapter Thirteen

WHILE I DON'T DRINK any more champagne after all—Krim sticks close after we duck back into the crowds—the rest of the evening passes in a blur. I never do eat much, just circulate answering questions and scoping out the adults who may meet us in the Hunt.

There is a brief moment of shock when I suddenly come face to face with King Ilan and Queen Helena. Luckily, Sergeant Krim is there, intervening. He covers for me when I find myself tongue-tied, tossing out some casual comments about my preparation and skills when the rulers of Elleon ask about my Hunt prospects. At one point I look directly in the queen's eyes and shiver. My heart seems to want to wrench its way out of my chest at being so close to my real mother. My birth mother. Oma is my real mother and always will be. But this woman who gave birth to me, who gave me away...

Who saved my life, when as a royal twin—and the female one—I would have *disappeared*, permanently. She sent me into hiding.

Maybe someday I'll have the chance to ask her why she did it.

While the festivities the next morning don't start as early as the Hunt will on the following day, it's still difficult to drag ourselves out of bed and get to the stadium on time for our exhibition. The banquet ran into the early morning, and even if we're not hungover, every one of us is too tired to discuss the party over breakfast or during our run to the stadium.

When we arrive at the tunnel leading inside, Sergeant Krim stops us for a final talk. There are still four Purple Recruits who are in the dark, so he can't say anything about our plans for the Hunt itself. Nonetheless, we can read the meaning behind his words of encouragement.

"Today, you have the chance to make a name for yourselves before the Hunt begins. Everyone here wants to see how you perform, to judge your levels of skill and fitness." He pauses, looking around at our faces. "You will do your best and make me proud. I want to walk out of this stadium with my head held high, knowing that I have trained the best group of Recruits the Transcendent Hunt will ever see."

There are a bunch of new corporals waiting to assist with the day's activities. They hand each of us a tag to pin to our uniforms.

"These monitors will record your efforts electronically," Sergeant Krim says. "We want to make sure there are no errors in scoring. They also record your vital signs, to see how well your body is handling the stress of combat." He pauses, looking intently at each of us. "Remember at all times that your efforts are being recorded."

Sometimes it's not what he says that matters, but rather the meaning beneath his words. Krim is warning us. I look down as one of the corporals attaches the monitor to my chest. Our efforts will be recorded. And no doubt our words will be, as well. I glance up from the purple badge displaying my name above a field of blinking lights, catching the sergeant's eyes. He nods slowly. He's seen that I understand. I dip my chin in response and turn away.

With that, he turns and leads us inside and onto the field.

Cheers erupt from the thousands of spectators in the stands. They may be spectators today, but many of them will be participating in the Hunt tomorrow. How can they be so cheerful, so excited, as if this is all a game? Tomorrow they expect to kill many of the Sixteens I've come to know as friends.

Is this what a blood-stratified society makes of ordinary human beings?

Monsters, who think it's a sport to hunt down other people?

At the far end of the stadium, a royal pavilion of gold-embroidered purple silks shades the thrones of King Ilan and

Queen Helena. Beside them, on a smaller but no-less-ornate chair, sits a boy. Prince Hern.

I have hardly spared a thought for my long-separated twin since I discovered the truth of my origins. Yet there he sits, my brother. The reason for my exile.

There's hardly time to consider what Prince Hern means to me. Is he a monster, too, like these others from Mag City? He never had to have his blood Tested. He was born royal, so when he took the treatment, they knew his blood would be *Lorem Sanguis*. A mixture of Red, Purple, and Blue, suspended in a clear matrix. The mark of his worthiness to rule Elleon when his father passed on.

When *our* father passed on.

I wonder if, given the chance, he would be standing here today. So many things are hidden from me, even now that I know what I am. But there's no time to think about that. I turn my thoughts to what lies before us and focus on the exhibition.

Across the field, there are stations marked out on the grass where we will rotate through the demonstrations of our skills. Sergeant Krim counts us off and sends us in small groups to the different areas. I'm assigned to the *joong bong* staff area for my first match. But before the demonstrations begin, we have to listen to "encouraging words" from the dais.

It's not the king or queen who steps up to the microphone this time.

It's Prince Hern.

Seeing him so clearly—hearing him speak—makes it difficult for me to focus on his words. His voice is not as deep as I expect, looking at his dark good looks. He doesn't seem nervous at all, not like I would be if I had to speak in front of thousands of strangers. I wonder if it comes naturally, or if it's something he's learned.

One of the advantages of being born—and raised—royal.

Standing there on the field, waiting for the events of the day to get underway, listening to the Crown Prince speak, I have a sudden revelation. If things had been different, if I hadn't been a twin, it could be me up there. I could have been the Crown Princess. When King Ilan dies I could have become Queen Kairyn, and ruled Elleon.

I could have changed this vile Transcendent Hunt, the entire blood caste system our society revolves around, and made this a far better country for everyone. Although, I have to wonder if I would have had the perspective born of living through this as an outsider, as someone from far beyond the reach of "civilized" society.

I wonder if my brother would do the same.

I wonder what kind of a king he will be, someday.

“Welcome, everyone, to the Transcendent Hunt,” Prince Hern says into the microphone. “This great event was begun by our ancestors, in ancient days, to provide a way for those among us without the advantage of superior Blood to gain an advantage beyond the lives they were born to, to move up in society and prove themselves worthy of a better life. But it benefits everyone, Purple and Blue Bloods alike. As you know,” he looks down at the stack of white cards he holds in his hand, where the words of his speech are written, “for those not born in Mag City, there is a lot to learn about how our society functions. The Transcendent Hunt also allows new Purples to find their place among us, based on their own performance.”

Prince Hern glances up, his eyes surveying the event stations and those of us soon to demonstrate our skills. As his gaze passes over the *joong bong* area, I catch his eyes for a long moment and see...

Sadness? Tiredness? Resignation?

Maybe he isn’t quite so enamored of Purple society as one would expect.

“Viewers in the stands, please be sure to vote for your favorite participants,” Hern goes on. He seems a little sad now, his face sagging. How odd. “As you know, this year governmental representatives have returned to each of the communities throughout Elleon, to share the Transcendent Hunt preparations. While viewers in our fine communities won't be able to see the Hunt itself, they are even now gathered in their own meeting halls to watch today's events on screens set up just for this purpose, so that they can cheer on their own participants."

While there is general applause throughout the stadium, on the field we are completely silent, looking around at each other in shock. I look around, spotting River in the fencing area. Our eyes meet, catch, hold. We are thinking the same thing.

Right now, in Eie, our parents are sitting in the meeting barn on folding chairs, watching us prepare to meet our deaths. I wonder what Oma is feeling, knowing what she does about me. I wonder if she is sitting surrounded by the Council members, or if she is being ostracized for raising a daughter who is expected to kill her best friend.

Mallen and Liiken.

"Sixteens, how about a wave for your families back home?"

Although he says it with enthusiasm, Prince Hern looks like he wants to vomit. He knows what is to come. And I am sure he is not in favor. Maybe there is some hope that he will end this atrocity once he is king.

That doesn't help us now, of course.

"And now, I hereby declare the 187th Elleon Transcendent Hunt open. Let the demonstration of skills begin!" Hern retreats from the microphone to uproarious applause. In front of the stage beneath the purple silks wafting so gracefully in the morning breeze, a pair of blue-uniformed trumpeters lift their instruments to their lips and blow a long, drawn-out note before stepping back.

At each station spaced out across the field, military attendants begin giving instructions and lining us up to compete. I don't recognize the corporal assigned to the *joong bong* staff, but she seems to know what she's doing. I am paired with a Blue boy named Zave. I've trained with him before, so I know his style.

While Zave and I wait our turn on the raised platform to show off our skills, I take the opportunity to look around, to see what further intel I can gather. Behind us, at the opposite end of the field from the Royal pavilion, a huge scoreboard has risen out of the ground with each of our names on it in bright purple or blue lights. Columns follow our names: Skill, Style, and Overall. But after the last column there are two others, with abbreviations I can't work out. *Agg*, and *Brt*.

Try as I might, I can't figure out what those are for.

Looking around the stands, I see that our audience has a flat pad mounted on the back of the seat in front of each of them, similar to what Krim uses to take notes on. The audience members' fingers fly over these small screens. Out of the corner of my eye,

I see numbers begin to flash on the huge scoreboard behind us, appearing beside the names of the first participants at each demonstration station.

I look closer, trying to puzzle it out.

After the *Overall* column, there are two more with no headings. Numbers begin to appear there too. Our overall scores? But, no, there's a heading for that. What does this last number signify?

Competitor	**Comm.**	**Skill**	**Style**	**Agg**	**Brt**	**Overall**		
Wadyn - Purple	Mey						3:1	100,000
Emvy - Blue	Elm						20:1	35,000
Kairyn - Purple	Eie						5:1	80,000
Dantil - Blue	Ara						12:1	63,000
Geia - Blue	Mey						7:1	75,000
Karia - Purple	Ava						10:1	50,000
Nria - Blue	Aia						17:1	41,500
Bren - Purple	Moz						6:1	78,000
River - Blue	Eie						9:1	53,500

Although the demonstrations have barely started, numbers continue rolling across that last column. It seems vital that I figure out what those final columns mean, but before I can figure it out, I feel a presence at my shoulder. Without looking, I can tell it's Sergeant Krim. There's something about him I'm beginning to know quite well.

Too well.

Without looking back, I ask, "What are those abbreviations, *Agg* and *Brt*? And the last two columns?"

Krim speaks quietly, but I can't tell if he's trying to keep it from everyone else. "*Agg* stands for 'aggressiveness.' And *Brt* is 'brutality.'"

Amidst the brilliant blue skies and colorful crowd and activity on the field, everything seems to go quiet. I can't believe that those are factors in the scoring. Such cold-bloodedness. That's not the worst of it, though. Krim clears his throat and leans in closer, leaving barely a breath of space between us. He speaks directly into my ear. "Of the unmarked columns, the first is the odds column. They're placing bets on you, on which of you will survive."

My blood—my damned *Lorem Sanguis* royal blood—runs cold.

They place odds on our *survival*? I've never heard of this.

Why haven't I heard of this?

The Purple Bloods of Mag City place bets on our lives. This is no longer just Purples against Blues, fighting for survival. These monsters find pleasure in profiting from our living or dying. They aren't our fellow humans after all. They are barbarians.

I don't think I want to know now, but I ask him anyway. "And the last?"

"The last signifies the amount of money whoever kills you will receive. The amounts are higher for newly-Tested Purples," he says, barely a whisper of air moving against my ear. "That's how we weed out those unworthy of rising into our exalted ranks." I swear I can hear the nausea in his voice. He really despises this whole thing.

It's no wonder he's on our side.

I whip my head around, meeting Sergeant Krim's hooded eyes. He is a full head taller than me, so I have to tilt my head back, exposing my throat. If he were an animal, he could rip out my trachea with just one bite.

Our eyes catch. Hold. My lips part, ready to speak, to shout my outrage, but his finger is there, covering my mouth, sealing the words inside.

"Not now," he says softly. "Remember the tech."

And I do remember. The badges we wear pinned to our chests have all kinds of sensors. My heartrate has no doubt skyrocketed. I take a deep breath, another, and yet again, feeling my pulse begin to slow. If we needed any further proof that we were expendable—Sixteens of either Blood color—here it is.

That final column seals our fate.

Or it did, in years past. This time, the Transcendent Hunt is about to take a turn in our favor.

When it is my turn to meet my opponent on the raised platform, I grip my staff loosely, easily. Zave rushes in with a flurry of moves. Showy, but wasting energy. I circle him, meeting every blow of his wooden staff, watching the numbers beside our names flicker, changing with every blow. A plan is beginning to form, but it will take the day to lay it out.

Krim said when we arrived at the stadium that he expected us to do our very best today, to make him proud. I know that the better we each perform today, the higher our rankings will rise. We'll be more attractive targets for those Purples who want to make a name for themselves, or to earn a bigger payout when they kill us.

I plan to be the most attractive target of us all.

The more pursuers I attract, the easier it will be for the others to escape serious injury or death. If my companions pick off the less-dangerous opponents, they can then turn and come after my pursuers, taking them down en masse. My strategy is beginning to form.

Throughout the day, with weapon after weapon, I defeat my fellow Sixteens. I watch the scoreboard as my numbers begin to rise. By the end of the day, my odds are ranked at 2:1, the lowest of any Sixteen here. And my payout has risen to 1.6 million dollars.

Despite my showy performance, I am proud to know that none of my opponents has suffered more than minor bruising. They will all be fit to compete for their very lives tomorrow. And at the end of the day, I am the leader, as I planned.

Now, to let the others know my plan to survive the next day. *All* of the others. Because I know now that even the four who haven't joined our ranks are going to be swept up in this plot, or they, too, may lose their lives.

And I'm not letting any of my fellow Sixteens die needlessly.

Chapter Fourteen

"THAT LAST COLUMN ON the scoreboard signifies how much money your killer will get, or—if you somehow manage to defeat everyone who comes at you—how much money you walk away with." Sergeant Krim's eyes are cold. He needs to maintain some kind of distance, even though I know he's determined to see each of us succeed.

But he's not explaining it clearly enough, I'm afraid.

We're all gathered in the Purple section of the dormitory after lights out, Blue Bloods perched beside Purples on their cots, leaning against the walls between the beds, or sitting cross-legged on the floor. Krim is leaning up against the windowsill, arms folded across his chest, trying to offer us final words of advice for tomorrow.

I stand up from my bed and move into the narrow aisle between the rows of cots.

No one has been left out of this meeting, not even the four Purples who have proved untrustworthy, eager to toe the line and play the game as the original instigators intended. Sergeant Krim didn't like it, but I was adamant.

"What the Sergeant means is that whoever kills me," I look around at everyone, "will walk away with over a million and a half. Now, you saw how I performed today. Do any of you think you can take me down?" The dropped eyes tell me all I need to know about their belief in their prospects. They know they can't take me, and probably none of the adults can, either. "If today had been the real thing, I would be as rich as Prince Hern right now." I glance over at Sergeant Krim again. He knows what I'm getting at, although none of my fellow Sixteens ever will. "Not only would I have that million and a half for surviving the Hunt. I would also have all of the money for defeating each of you. That's what I want you to focus on, those people betting on us today."

Krim's eyes narrow. I haven't had a chance to tell him about my plan before. He probably had his suspicions, but he's about to find out just how devious I can be.

"Everyone who was in the stadium today thinks that I am the one to beat. To kill. I made sure they'd all be coming after me. Or most of them, anyway. But if we work together, we can all survive."

River has been sitting on the farthest bed from the door, near Krim, his head sunken into his chest. He's exhausted. But now he raises his head, shaking the shaggy hair back out of his eyes, and stares at me in shock. “So that’s why you were so...so...”

“Indomitable is the word you’re looking for, River,” the sarge says. “I was wondering.” He steps away from the window and stares directly at me. “What is your plan, Corporal Kairyn?”

Corporal Kairyn. I’ve gained in rank, even if it’s not official.

I look at the four Purples who haven’t been brought over to our side until now, knowing the others will be ready to follow my lead. These four, however, need to be convinced. I think back to the military history we’ve been learning here. I remember a famous saying from the country we used to be, before the Blood War gave birth to Elleon. “United we stand, divided we fall. Right? We are all going to fight for our lives together, united. There’s no reason for us to kill each other, just to fulfill some archaic societal standard. If we remain strong together, there’s no reason for any of us to die. And we’ll all profit from the Hunt, instead of the adults making money off our corpses.”

I seek out the four Purple holdouts—Wadyn and his twin Radyn, the brother and sister from Mel, Del from Eos, and Heryd from Ara, two more boys who thought the Hunt was their way to find a place in Mag City society—meeting and holding their gazes until their eyes drop. I still don’t think they’re 100% convinced to join us, though.

"Look, the way this works is that an adult who kills one of us gets the bounty—that number that was in the last column—for taking us down. But we get a bounty for each adult we take out. And it's us or them. So, if we work together, we all profit from the Hunt, as well as walking out alive. And I, for one, am willing to split my bounty forty-seven ways. That's at least $34,000 for each of you, just for helping me stay alive."

Wadyn leans back on his sister's bed, propping himself up on his elbows. "Yeah, but if I kill you, I get 1.6 million dollars. Why wouldn't I go for you straight out of the gate?"

"Because," I say, figuring quickly, "if you help with this plan, you'll get not just a forty-seventh of my bounty, but also of everyone else's, which is way more than mine alone. And you don't have to worry about any of us gunning for you, or Radyn."

The bounties on Purples had turned out to be higher than Blues, because apparently we had a higher value in Mag City society, even though we had just Tested Purple and hadn't found a place in their ranks yet.

"Kai's right," Jeaol, the Purple boy from Elm who won the *parkour* challenges a couple weeks ago, steps in. "I've figured it out. If we all survive, we each walk away with over $2,000,000, more depending on how many adults we take out."

After a couple more minutes of discussion, they reach a consensus. "Okay, so what do we do?" Wadyn asks. It's reassuring to see that he's come around, as have the other three.

I nod to him, and smile at Radyn. She's the weaker of the twins, combat-wise. I have no doubt that's played into her twin's agreement.

"So, today I gave it everything I had to make me look good and you all," I look around the dorm at my fellow Sixteens, "as weak as possible."

"You sure did that!"

"Don't I know it!"

"You mean I'm not really that pathetic?"

The chorus of comments is rueful, rather than offended. A good sign. They're on my side now.

I smile. "The higher my bounty climbed, the more adults there would be coming for me," I say. "That means that the rest of the adults, the not-so-great fighters, will go for you. The numbers will be in our favor. There are a hundred adults registered for the Hunt, which is a little over two of them to each of us. If twenty or thirty come after me, that means the odds are nearly halved. If we work together, pair up and watch each other's backs, then we take out those weaker ones and clear the field. Then all of you come after the adults who are chasing me and work together to eliminate them."

I notice then that Jaoan, a Blue boy from Moz, has tears streaming down his cheeks. One of the Purples, Raeve from Aia, drops down on the bed beside him and wraps his arms around Jaoan's shoulders, pulling him close. Raeve looks at me challengingly.

"We...we never thought we could—" Raeve can't quite force the words out, but we all know what he's trying to say.

Romance was supposedly forbidden in the barracks, but in such close quarters...

This is an unexpected development.

The story of Mallen and Liiken has spread beyond the borders of Eie to become a cautionary tale among all of the communities. All these weeks of them training together, falling in love, having that bitter ending hanging over their heads. Poor Jaoan and Raeve were training together, knowing they could never *be* together.

Now, there is hope not just for all of us to survive, but to thrive. If we can just find our way through this.

"Are we agreed, then?"

All of them are in.

Chapter Fifteen

BEFORE WE BROKE UP last night, Sergeant Krim had pulled out a map of the course and gone over it in detail. An added advantage, and one we could use. The Transcendent Hunt begins at daybreak and ends that evening. Twelve hours. And we have a lot of ground to cover in between.

The sky is barely lightening along the eastern horizon when the transport buses arrive at the Hunting grounds. We are on the edge of the reclaimed lands to the west of Mag City. In front of us lie forest and fields, bombed areas complete with the wreckage of ancient buildings and huge bomb craters, as well as a couple of abandoned towns and one medium-sized city from before the Blood War.

The finish line is over ten miles away, over this harsh terrain. The course runs through former farmland and forest, small towns and residential areas, ending up three miles inside a small, ruined city called Springfield at a building called the Lincoln Home, from the time before the Blood War. To win their freedom, the Blues need to reach this goal. The rest of us just need to survive, to stay alive. But today we will all reach the end, together.

Alive.

The road we are on ends just ahead of us, winding into an overgrown area where the trees have rooted in the macadam, tearing it apart as years passed without maintenance of any kind. There are several large tents set up on what remains of the formerly level surface of the road. Inside one I see long tables loaded with armaments. Firearms of all the kinds we've trained with fill one table, blades—including swords, machetes, and knives—are lined up on another. A smaller table off to one side boasts ammunition to load the firearms, while there are stacks of armored vests and helmets beside it.

"All right, Sixteens," Sergeant Krim herds us from the buses to the weapons tent. "Choose your weapons. Take whatever you need but remember that whatever you take adds to your load. You've got ten miles of rough terrain to cover before the day is through. Every ounce you pack in is going to slow you down."

A chill runs down my spine at his matter-of-fact tone of voice. We're about to enter the fight of our lives. On the ride out here, we discussed the best strategies for survival. Everyone agreed that while we needed to work together, we can go one step further. Everyone paired up with a partner, to work together to reach the finish line. Everyone except me, the odd one out. But I'd already planned to lead away the majority of our enemies, to free up the others. Once the larger number of our foes were out of sight and hearing, the paired-up Purple and Blue Sixteens will circle back and come in behind, taking the Hunters down.

Krim moves to the table of vests and helmets, picking up one of the camouflage-patterned garments. "Everyone gets a vest. These will automatically send back your vitals, so that we can track your progress. The monitor here," he points out a tech device on the front upper chest area, "tells us if you're alive or dead, what your heart rate and BP are, what your oxygen levels are. There's also a clock to keep track of your time and a pedometer for distance traveled. Each of you are tracked by GPS so that any kills you make will be credited to your account. And if you're wounded, punch here," he points to a round red button, "to signal for pickup. A med team will respond and if you're still alive, they'll carry you off the field. Keep the vest on at all times."

There's one other thing we all settled on, which Sergeant Krim doesn't know about. Everyone agreed that becoming killers ourselves wasn't who we wanted to be. We'd take out our foes if absolutely necessary. But if it was possible—and safe—we would capture and restrain the adult Hunters, using the supply of zip ties each of us carries in the large pockets of our fatigues.

River is the one to ask the question we've probably all been thinking about. "Sarge? What if we don't kill, but only wound? Will we get the bounty then?"

"Yes, but it will be reduced by the severity of the wound. We don't need to go into all that now. The one thing you need to focus on is staying alive. And reaching the finish line." Krim pauses consideringly, then—decision reached—speaks again. "If you don't reach the finish line, if you decide to just take cover in the countryside and wait it out, you collect nothing. Remember this: the Hunt is meant to sort the weak from the strong, and strength is everything in Elleon. Physical strength, yes, but mental strength as well. Skill, cleverness, the ability to think on your feet. You can survive the day but end up cleaning sewers for the rest of your life. The bounties you score, which are credited when you reach the finish line, are what will set you up for the rest of your lives."

So much to think about. But I'm not worried. I will reach the finish line. We all will if our plan succeeds.

In the cover of heavy trees, long-distance rifles won't serve much purpose, so I pass over those and select a 9mm handgun, a small revolver for backup, and a small bow with a quiver of short arrows. I also choose three knives I can conceal on my body: a morphing karambit, a ghostrike, and a KA-BAR TDI. I add a 10-inch hunting knife in a belt sheath, useful not just for stabbing, but also for cutting staffs from small trees if needed.

Once I'm armed to my satisfaction, I head outside. Under a large tree are stacks of camo backpacks, prefilled with supplies for the day's trek. Several bottles of water, energy bars, and a first-aid kit fill the packs, each one identical. As I'm double checking my equipment, several more buses pull up, parking along the side of the crumbling road.

When the doors open, the Transcendent Hunters begin to pile out, already loaded down with their own personal arms and equipment. Their outfits look expensive, camouflage uniforms tightly fitted in some stretchy fabric, shiny leather boots, and tech gadgets hanging from their belt loops.

While we wait for the signal to begin the Hunt, several of the adult Purples compare their weapons. A couple of them raise rifles to their shoulders and begin firing off into the forest. We hadn't planned for this. They will see that their weapons don't work—thanks to our sabotage—and we'll be exposed.

But that's not what happens.

Leaves fly from trees and bark is blasted from the trunks. The Purples' weapons—which we worked so hard to disable—are working.

Our sabotage has been countermanded. I suddenly realize that in spite of our planning, we are severely outmatched. Not only have the official weapons been repaired, but they have more tech that we never saw. How is that fair?

I'm afraid that fair has nothing to do with the Hunt.

"All right, Sixteens! Form up!"

With everyone fully armed, we gather around Sergeant Krim on one side, away from the adult Hunters. Looking around, I can see that each pair has chosen a variety of weapons that complement their partner's, enough to cover any eventuality. Now, we just have to remember how to use these tools to keep ourselves alive.

"You will have a ten minute head start," the sarge is saying as I focus my attention on him again. He meets my eyes and nods slightly, twitching his eyes to the left. That's where I'll enter the tree line. "Be smart, be safe, and make me proud. Go!"

I cut left, separating myself from the rest of the pack. The adult Hunters are lined up across the clearing and as I run across the broken pavement, I glance over at them, a challenge in my eyes. Many of them meet my gaze and I grin as they track me visually. Good.

Crashing into the underbrush beneath the first row of oaks and maples, I hurdle fallen logs and push through a tangle of blackberry shrubs, heavy with fruit in the late summer's rising heat. I hadn't realized how noisy it was back in the arrival area, but once in the woods silence descends, peaceful, broken only by the sounds of birdsong and my fellow Sixteens racing away from me.

I haven't felt this kind of peace since leaving Eie. It reminds me of growing up in the untouched countryside, climbing trees and swimming in the stream. A thought hovers in the folds of my mind, off to one side. I finally allow it to surface, but only for a wisp of a moment before I force it back into hiding.

Will I ever see Eie again?

I set a swift, yet steady pace, one I can maintain for hours if need be. I don't want to get too far ahead, though. If they lose my trail, the adults may start looking for the other Sixteens. I might return to Eie, but at a cost I'll never be able to live with.

As I move through the still, early morning air, I keep scanning the territory for natural advantages. If a Hunter gets too close, I need to find a defensive position, where I can hold them off or take them out. The ground's pretty low this close to the old road, but rises a little way ahead, if I remember Sergeant Krim's map correctly. Higher ground is good, from a firing standpoint. I can also climb a tree, hiding in a leafy nest to shoot an opponent. And there are low rocky outcroppings poking through the leaf mold on the forest floor, which I know will get bigger the farther I get from the road.

When I check the monitor attached to my vest, eight minutes have passed. Time to start moving smart, instead of fast. I still need to get to the finish line, to keep moving forward.

The ground begins to rise and through the trees I can see a shadow of gray. Within minutes I reach the first rocky outcropping, rising abruptly out of the ground. I skirt to the right, following the head-high granite until I find a narrow fold in the rock I can climb, wedging the soles of my boots into the crevice. When I reach the top, I stop to catch my breath. Dropping my pack to the ground, I pull out an energy bar and gobble down a large piece, then chug down half a bottle of water.

As I lift the bottle to my lips, I realize my hand is shaking slightly. Exertion? Adrenaline? I am racing for my life.

Will our plan work?

Will everyone play their parts?

I've never had to put my faith in so many uncontrollable variables before, to trust that someone else won't mess up and let me down. That's a frightening thing.

I check my clock again. Eighteen minutes have passed. The adult Hunters are definitely on their way through the forest behind us, drawing closer with every fleeting second. This is a good vantage point, a defensible hide, where I can shoot down on anyone coming through the forest behind me. I know I can't afford the time to wait here and see who shows up, though. With a sigh of resignation, I shrug into my pack again and race off, boot heels ringing across the ancient rock.

Without warning, a shot rings out in the trees behind me, and I drop into a crouch. The shot wasn't that close, so the Hunter wasn't firing at me. Another of my companions may be injured right now. Or dead.

Best case, they've taken out an opponent.

I won't think about whether a Sixteen just killed another human being or wounded them. These questions have no place in warfare. We are going to do things we never expected when we were innocent kids growing up in the outer communities. I push down my moral quandaries.

Your only limit is you. Be fearless.

I move on.

The ground begins to drop again, leading down into a valley slicing through the forest. A stream runs below, narrow enough to cross. As I'm jumping down into the rushing water, I hear a noise behind me and drop down behind the root ball of a large tree, up to my waist in the freezing cold water as I wriggle in beneath the concealment of the snaking roots.

Within moments, I hear the crack of a twig, the rustle of leaves, just above my head. I squirm tighter in beneath the root ball, making sure my pack is completely hidden. I barely breathe, waiting...

I don't have long to wait. Within seconds, I see a pair of boots jump into the stream just beyond my hiding place. As they move away, I can see that it's a large man, overweight really. I remember him from the clearing. He was one of the most heavily-loaded with high-tech devices and massive weapons. I'd thought then that—remembering Krim's warning about weight—this guy would exhaust himself with all of the stuff he was carrying. He didn't seem to be struggling, though. Not yet anyway. Despite the rolls of fat across his gut, I have no doubt he could take me out without breaking a sweat.

Thank the gods I found a hiding place just in time.

His tree-trunk sized legs stomp across the width of the stream and I'm ready to leap out of concealment and run as soon as he's out of sight. But barely seconds later another pair of boots splash down into the stream, and another. They're hunting in a pack, like wolves.

As if there aren't real wolves somewhere in this forest to worry about. Wolves and coyotes and bears and—

This isn't doing me any good. I need to stay focused on the real threat, the most dangerous animal of all.

Humans.

The Hunters—five in all—are moving quickly to ford the stream, weapons at the ready.

I'm going to need to be smart now, not just swift.

As they leave the stream and move out of sight into the forest, I pull myself out from beneath the root ball, soaked to the skin and shivering. In the cover of the trees, the sun barely reaches the ground. I'll dry as I run, though. A little discomfort is nothing compared to being killed.

I follow behind the five Hunters, close enough to hear the faint sounds of them moving through the underbrush just out of sight. The summit of a rise from the lower-level stream grows ahead and I can see the back of the last Hunter disappear from view. It's a woman, again with the most expensive-looking gear. Dodging from tree to tree, I follow her up the hill.

When I reach the top, the five Hunters have spread out, heading downwards again. The geometric angles of ruined houses poke through the trees, spreading out for a mile or more, the intermittent remains of a small town destroyed in the Blood War. Narrow paths run between the ruins, former roads which tied the community together.

I move carefully into the cover of the overgrown foliage that has taken over the town. I know there are five Hunters in front of me, but I have no idea who's coming up behind me. I have no doubt that there are more coming. My senses are all on high alert for the slightest sound, the barest sign of movement.

I drop into a crouch behind a tangle of wild rose vines growing up the trunk of a pine tree, the flowers losing pink petals with every lift of the morning breeze. Although I am a quick draw, this is too close to proceed without a weapon in my hand.

Silently, I pull the 9mm from my holster, cradling the metal in my hand.

A small sound alerts me to the presence of another living being close by. *Too* close. There's a crumbling brick wall about eight feet ahead, just tall enough for a person to hide behind and lie in wait for their prey. I sight toward the wall, staring down the barrel of my weapon. Within moments a loud rustling sounds. I prepare to fire a leg shot to disable, not kill. Luckily, by aiming lower, I see the creature before I fire. It's just a large badger, scurrying out from behind the wall. I release the breath I've been holding in a *whoosh*.

I haven't had to defend myself yet, but I can't relax.

Lowering my gun hand, I wipe sweat from my forehead. I've never been faced with shooting another human before. This is going to be difficult. I need to get past those qualms, right now. I won't have a choice but to shoot someone, not if I'm going to survive the day.

Still holding my weapon at the ready, I move out from behind the concealment of the rose vines, raising my arm to brush away a few pink petals clinging to my sleeve. *Whap*! Shocked, I see the fletching feathers of an arrow sticking out of the tree trunk just below my elbow.

In an instant, three things happen. I realize that if I hadn't raised my arm to brush away the rose petals, I would have been nailed to the tree trunk by the high-powered arrow. I pivot and fire in the direction the arrow came from, hitting a man concealed on top of one of the rotting house's roofs. And as the man tumbles to the ground, I drop and roll further into the overgrown plantings of what had once been a formal garden, squirming beneath an old concrete bench, half buried in rotting leaves.

Whispers rise nearby, too quiet to make out the words, but loud enough for me to pinpoint the locations of the other four Hunters. They're spaced out across an open, grassy area. The old street along which the houses are positioned. Reaching behind my back, I unhook my own short bow, knocking an arrow into the string and pulling back, holding it at the ready. I raise the bow slowly, silently, sighting past the curved carbon-fiber bow, alert for any movement.

Maybe it's my royal blood that gives me steely nerves and good eyesight. I see the bare whisper of movement of leaves about seventy feet away, across the street, and lose my arrow silently.

"*Oomph*!" The leader of the pack of Hunters I've followed from the stream tried to sneak toward the man I'd already shot, and my arrow takes him in the shoulder. I see the flash of camo against rotting wood as he falls backwards, sprawling across what had once been the front porch of a suburban home.

"Oppina! Help me!" he cries out.

I can see him clutching at his shoulder as he tries to squirm back into cover, looking like a turtle flipped on his back. Another of the Hunters, the woman that had been at the end of the line as I pursued them, scurries out of cover and onto the porch, taking cover behind an old column and reaches out to check the man's wound.

"Oppina! Help me!" he cries out again.

I see the woman survey the area. She can't tell where the arrow came from. Good for me. She turns back to the man, in one movement slipping a long knife from a sheath at her belt and slitting his throat, leaving him gurgling in his own blood as the life drains from his body.

I shudder. I thought that we were going to need to be ruthless today to survive this Hunt. But this is true ruthlessness. Killing one of your own. She probably thought it would slow them down to have to take time to care for the wounded man.

There's been no more movement from the man I shot on the roof, so I'm pretty sure he's dead, too. That's two out of one hundred.

I wonder how the other Sixteens are doing. Are they thinning the Hunters' numbers? Or are they falling to the adults' attacks?

But I need to concentrate on my own efforts and stop worrying about the others. We laid our plans. There's nothing more I can do for them.

I continue to follow the remaining three adult Hunters through the ruined town and out into the countryside again. In the overgrown meadows—former farm fields—I veer north of them, while they keep to the old roads. The going is harder for me, but from a distance, I can watch as other Hunters join up with them, and then peel away. Sharing intel, no doubt.

When they enter a heavily wooded area, I shift in closer, to keep them in sight, flanking them. I need to take more of them out, thin the herd so that I can reach the finish line, and so that they aren't able to Hunt down the others. As I top a small rise, I spot tree limbs rustling about five hundred yards in front of the group of adult Hunters, which has now grown to ten or eleven. Silently, I creep closer, keeping low.

Sudden gunfire rings out, bullets peppering the forest. The Hunters scatter, taking cover behind wide tree trunks. This is old-growth forest, here before the war. The trees are massive, total protection from an attack. I drop to the ground, shouldering out of my pack, leaving it behind as I squirm closer through the underbrush. Peering ahead into the shadowed trees, I spot River, about twenty feet up in the concealing boughs of a hemlock tree. To his right, about ten yards away, his partner Elidys is behind a broad tree trunk, sighting down the barrel of a machine gun. And another fifty feet past her is Heryd, up a pine tree, and Karia, both Purples, on the ground beneath his feet.

Their relative positions are in a crescent, like a reverse half-moon with River farthest away in front of the adult Hunters.

Heryd was one of the four Purples who weren't brought in on the plan until last night. I've worried about those four, unsure if they were trustworthy. Now I know that I was right to worry. As I watch, Heryd raises a sniper rifle to his shoulder, sighting through the scope to find River.

My *Lorem Sanguis* blood freezes in my veins. This is it for all five of us. I ignore the eleven adult Hunters hiding behind tree trunks and focus on Heryd, sliding my 9mm back into the holster and drawing my bow. I won't hit anything at this distance, I'm still over 60 yards away. Maybe the sound alone will take the focus to give River enough time to get out of the way.

I feel helpless, but I can't let Heryd shoot River.

Sighting on Heryd's forehead, I am ready to release the arrow. Only to see him dip the end of the barrel in a signal, then swing the sniper rifle around, sighting through the trees.

He *is* working with River and Elidys.

Shaking, I realize I almost killed one of my companions. The damned government has made it impossible for us to trust one another, pitting one blood color against the other.

I hate this. It has to end.

All I can do now, though, is carry through with our plan. I draw my bow again, rising up behind the concealment of a thick stand of rhododendrons. Using the bow may not be as rapid fire as a gun, but the silence is a plus. The adults won't be able to follow the noise and start firing in my direction. But my arrows will be a distraction for the others, giving them an advantage.

From my position, directly behind the adults hiding behind the tree trunks, I have a perfect vantage point for my attack. I knock my first arrow and let it fly into the right arm of a woman with a rifle trained on the road ahead of her. She screams, pinned to the tree, dropping her rifle in a fusillade of bullets.

There's no time to see her rip the arrow from her flesh. River, Heryd, and the other two have opened fire. I see Hunters begin to fall, mostly under Heryd's attack, as well as Karia's, as they're off to the opposite side and the adults are in full view. Within moments the forest falls silent, except for the groans and sobbing of injured Hunters.

Moving silently, River, Elidys, and Heryd shimmy down from their perches in the trees and run towards their prey in a crouch, while Karia covers them. I run over to join them, pulling out a handful of zip ties.

"Nice teamwork, guys!" My voice is low. There may well be other Hunters nearby. In fact, I'm sure there are, fully expecting a bullet to rip into my back as I crouch over a wounded man to secure his arms behind his back. After punching the red button on his chest plate for "wounded: pickup," I look around at everyone. "You all good?"

Heryd moves closer, speaking quietly. "I saw you, out there," he gestures to where I was hiding on the edge of the overgrown fields. "You thought I was going to shoot River, didn't you?"

I freeze. I can't lie. Nodding, I look Heryd straight in the eyes. "I know him. I grew up with him. I don't know you."

He dips his head in acknowledgement. "And until last night, you didn't know if I was on your side or not. I get that." He pauses, looking away, but then his eyes flash back to my face. "But thanks for not shooting me. I've seen you with those things. I wouldn't stand a chance."

He grins, and I smile back.

Together, we're going to make it through this.

Together, but alone.

"I need to keep moving," I say as the other three come up to join us, having finished securing the wounded. "You guys be careful, okay? I'll see you at the end."

River steps forward to cut me off. I look at him, but I don't have time for this. He's on his own. Well, on his own with his other team members.

I am the one who's really alone here. In more ways than one.

I punch him in the shoulder, a gesture of friendship. "Be careful," I say, and slip away silently into the cover of the underbrush.

But I can feel his eyes on my back, even as I disappear behind the concealing leaves.

Chapter Sixteen

AS THE MORNING WANES and the sun reaches its zenith in the sky overhead, I run down my personal tally. Two dead in the ruined town, eleven wounded just beyond the meadows, and since then, fifteen more, by ones and twos. Except for the first two, I've managed to wound, not kill, for which I'm grateful. I don't know how I'd live with myself if I'd been forced to take all of those lives.

Directly ahead of me is an area marked off with barbed wire. There were signs here once, but they've rusted away to flakes of oxidation, lying in piles among the dead leaves. Beyond the barbed wire lies scrub land, weedy trees taking over whatever was here before, obliterating the past of our former civilization.

It will be a definite risk to bypass the barrier. Although this seems to be a former farming area, and this field probably just held a bull or something, there's no telling what remains of the Blood War might be hidden there.

It seems I have no choice. Repeated sounds of crashing and cursing are drawing ever closer. Whoever is on my trail now is not the most skilled of trackers, for which I'm grateful. They're easy to keep a bead on when they make so much noise. It seems that Elleon's lottery system for the Hunt participants works in our favor. Any adult can enter to win a place in the Hunt, to chase each year's Sixteens to the finish line.

Any adult *can* enter, and it seems they have, for amusement or glory. It doesn't matter how unskilled they are. Many of the opponents I've already taken down barely knew how to load their weapons, let alone aim and fire them. If I'd realized that fact beforehand, maybe I wouldn't have been so afraid.

Then again, being afraid has kept me sharp.

The lack of skill on the part of the adults is one secret I'm glad Sergeant Krim kept to himself.

The sounds of pursuit are closer now, louder. I crouch down and slip between the strands of barbed wire. Keeping low, I scurry deeper into the overgrown grass, head down so that I won't be spotted from behind. I move slowly, knowing that an unusual swishing of tall grass can also give my position away. My progress is steady, but even so, I've only gone about a hundred yards before I hear them reach the fence.

Dropping to my knees on the soft soil I turn, look back, my eyes barely above the tips of the grass stalks. There's a whole pack of adult Hunters lined up there. I count seventeen of them. And I know that they all want the 1.6 million for my corpse.

Our plan is working.

Heavy firepower, though. If they had the sense to unload their weapons on the field, laying down a barrage of bullets, I would be torn to shreds.

Luckily, they're not that smart. In a mass of enthusiasm, they begin to blunder their way through the strands of barbed wire. I drop lower and turn, moving faster, deeper into the field. It will be only moments before one—or more—of them stumbles across me and takes me down.

They seem to have spread out in a line the width of the field. Strategy. Maybe they're not so stupid after all. My breathing sharpens, almost panting. I need to keep calm, stay chill. Move. Move faster. Straight line. I don't have time to weave, and no one has spotted signs of my passing yet.

Blam!

The concussion throws me sprawling. I hug the ground, panting. Feel my limbs. All there. I lift a shaking hand to push back the hair from my eyes, looking around. Nothing. Nothing here.

In a flash of understanding, I realize that I've stumbled across an ancient minefield. Stumbled *into* a minefield. I'm lying prone in a minefield. Terrified, I freeze. I didn't set one off, so it must have been one of the adults chasing me. But there could be a mine nearby. I could be lying on one right now.

Behind me, all noise has ceased. I can't stay here. I have no choice. But no matter how careful I am, there's no way to know where the mines are buried. No signs after three hundred years, no scars in the earth from digging.

I have to take my chances.

I have to move. One step at a time.

Levering myself up from the ground on trembling legs, I rise to a crouch, pivot in place, and raise my head to see how close they are. A plume of dust blows away in the slight breeze, lifting over the swaying grass. Fifty yards, no, seventy-five yards away, behind and to my left. Sixteen remaining adult Hunters are frozen in place, spread out across the width of the field. They're smart enough to know what they've gotten into, but they can't figure out what to do now.

Just then the shouting starts. Someone screams a name. The one who died, no doubt. They're starting to look around. The Hunters have become the Hunted.

Right now, I could take them out, one by one, while they're too terrified to move. I'd have to do it quickly, too quickly. My weapons only fire one bullet at a time. If they stayed where they are, unmoving targets, I could do it. But as soon as I fire, they'll make a rush for cover. Some of them will join the one who just blew himself up, but some would get away. And I'd be a sitting duck.

I face the same danger from the buried mines that they do.

If only I had selected one of the larger rifles this morning, I could lay down a sweep of fire from one side of the field to the other, a couple of feet off the ground, hitting them in the legs.

Big mistake.

As I waste precious seconds regretting my choices, voices rise.

"What do I do?"

"How do we get out of here?"

"We're all going to die!"

I have the same choices that they do. And none of them are good. Only sheer luck will get me out of this alive. I pull my head down, pivot on the balls of my feet, and take one crouching step forward. Toward the other side. Toward another fence, somewhere out in front of me. How far? It doesn't matter. Wherever it is, I have to reach it to be safe. Another step. Another.

My breathing slows.

Step.

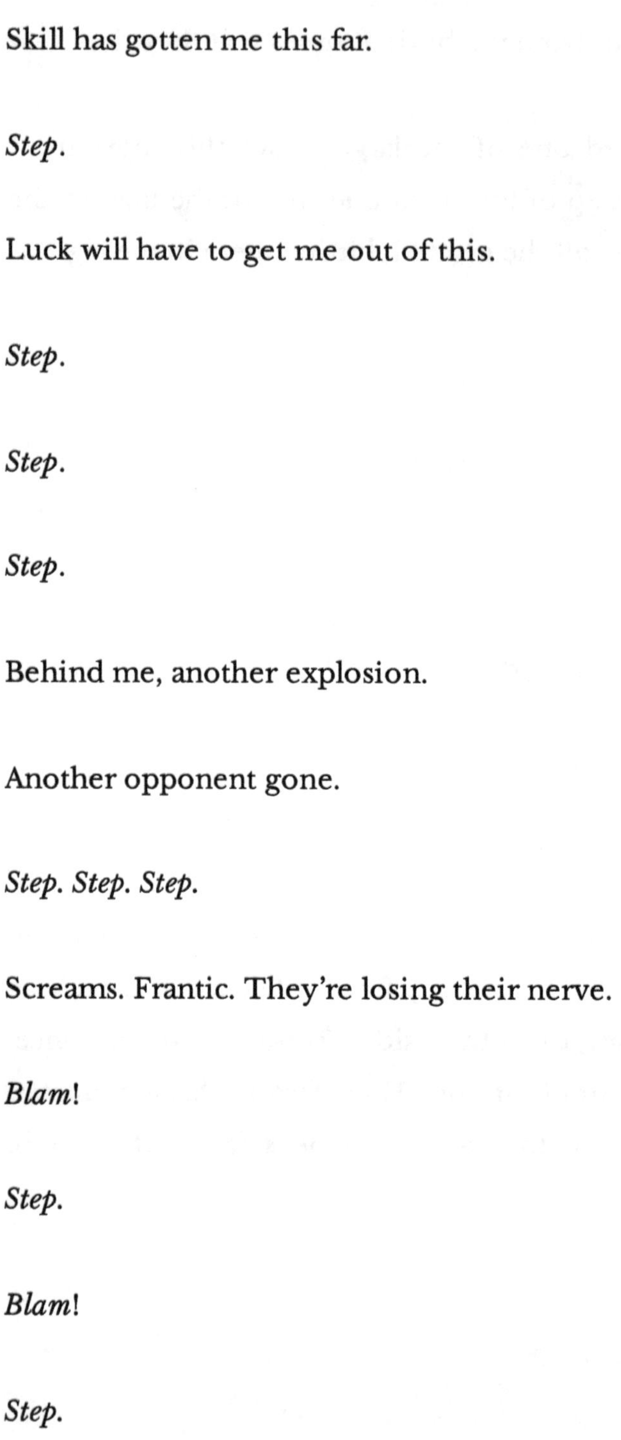

Skill has gotten me this far.

Step.

Luck will have to get me out of this.

Step.

Step.

Step.

Behind me, another explosion.

Another opponent gone.

Step. Step. Step.

Screams. Frantic. They're losing their nerve.

Blam!

Step.

Blam!

Step.

I count the concussions, not my steps. I don't need to know how far I've come.

I don't need to know how far to go.

I need to know how many Hunters are still on my trail.

Through the waving stalks of tall grass, it appears at last. The rusted wires of the fence. I've reached the other side.

Still alive.

How am I still alive?

I climb through the strands of barbed wire, legs shaking, soaked in sweat. Collapse onto the ground. Elbows on knees. Head in hands. Tears pouring down my face.

I'm still alive.

I counted fourteen explosions. Fourteen more enemies eliminated.

Fourteen more people dead, for no reason but to strike fear into the people of Elleon. To control the populace, force them to fear and hate each other.

This has to stop.

But first, I have to win this cruel, evil game. *We* have to win.

I pull a bottle of water from my pack and swallow half of it in one long gulp. I must stay hydrated; I'm losing too much in sweat. And the day isn't over yet.

Far-off shouts rise again from back near the trees on the other side of the field. I shoulder my pack again and stand, sighting over the field of tall grass stained red with the blood of my opponents. I can't claim those kills, which is a pity. I guess I'm losing my humanity, to be thinking like this. But the bounty payouts would buy a lot of weapons...

A shudder shakes my body from head to heels. Is this me? Am I thinking revolution? Although—

Who better?

I am of royal blood. I am *Lorem Sanguis.*

There are only two people standing between me and the throne of Elleon. King Ilan and Prince Hern. My father and my twin brother. Queen Helena doesn't count. My birth mother. She isn't in the direct line of succession. As I move away from the field of body parts, I realize I am plotting the overthrow of the monarchy. Of the entire government.

And those thoughts fuel my shaking legs as I set a steady pace through the ruined world of our ancestors. Toward the finish line. I've already started putting together an army, one comprised of forty-six other Sixteens. I've got my military commander in Sergeant Krim. He has already proven himself a subversive, conspiring to help us all survive this Hunt. He'll know who else we can bring in, some of his corporals, maybe, or other people in the military.

He will be invaluable.

Together we can bring down this corrupt government.

Krim and me.

Chapter Seventeen

BY THE TIME I reach the outskirts of the destroyed city I remember from Krim's map, my plans are taking shape. We will work together, Blues and Purples, to reform our world.

And there are Reds out there, somewhere in the wilderness. Reds like my friend Ulna, who fled Eie rather than submit to the corrective serum which turns Red blood to Blue and leaves the victims disfigured. They would fight with us.

Surveying the countryside leading up to the signs of former habitation, I see no movement. I keep to cover as much as possible, but I'm anxious to get through the city and reach the finish line on the other side. The remains of a road wind through overreaching trees, branches linked overhead to form a tunnel of green. I stick to the edge of the cracked macadam, scuttling through the underbrush like a possum.

At one point I spot the remains of a huge metal sign, marked with bullet holes and rust. There's the shadow of what looks like a portrait of a bearded man at the top, with rows of ornate lettering underneath. I step closer to try to make out the words.

"*Welcome to Springfield,*" I read, the words hushed in the tunnel of green. Where was Springfield, before the war? It's forbidden to learn about the world before, and all of the books and files have been destroyed. The founders of Elleon did everything they could to rewrite our world.

I will do everything I can to rewrite it again, to root out the discrimination and evil of Elleon's Blood Caste. But I won't force people to forget. I'll make them learn from our mistakes.

Birdsong is the only sound as I move further into the crumbled ruins of Springfield. Birds singing, crickets chirping, grasshoppers whirring, frogs croaking. As long as those sounds continue, I know I'm alone. I move lightly, but swiftly. The day is long, dusk only an hour or so away now.

The finish line.

While staying alive—and uninjured—is the ultimate goal of the Transcendent Hunt for a Sixteen, there is another rule I didn't focus on, but which now seems to be very important for achieving *my* ultimate goal, the one which has been forming in my head since the minefield. We collect bounties on the adult Hunters we kill or wound. My score is pretty high right now. When I reach the finish line, I stand to collect hundreds of thousands of dollars, if not a million or more. I'll also collect the bounty set on me, in yesterday's demonstration events. If all of us put our take together for the day, all of us Sixteens, we can invest that money in the seeds of our revolution.

But those thoughts need to wait. For now, I have to finish this damned Hunt.

Moving deeper into the ruined city of Springfield, I take note of every pile of rubble, every crumbling building, every twisted steel framework surrounded by piles of concrete. I begin to form a view of the city from above, in my mind's eye, as if I were a hawk soaring above the ruins. The remains of manmade structures are softened by foliage, the opportunistic trees, shrubbery, and other plants which overgrew their containment or grew from seeds dropped by wildlife.

The greenness can't cover up the truth of this place, however. This is not just the destruction of time. This city was bombed. This land is scarred.

And it may never heal, not in another hundred years, or a thousand. The deadliness of mankind will always lurk beneath the surface.

I take great care not to fall prey to the remains of humanity. Several times I am forced to skirt huge holes in the ground, vast pits hundreds of feet deep. A single step placed wrong—like in the minefield—could mean a broken leg or twisted ankle. I've come through the Hunt uninjured. So far, at least. I can't afford to lose time or make an easier target of myself by falling in a hole or being attacked by a hungry coyote or a black bear. Animals have come back to inhabit the places mankind left behind. Opportunistic. That's a law of nature.

If there's a hole, something will fill it.

I just have to make sure that something is not me.

The pedometer on my vest has registered two miles since I entered the city of Springfield. One more mile to go. I can't lose sight of the fact that everyone left in this competition is heading the same way, through the same terrain. My senses are on high alert.

I suddenly realize the green world has gone silent around me. I drop to my knees behind a head-high metal machine of some sort, with a cracked black glass panel in the front. There are three of these machines in a row, and I move down the line carefully, keeping low. There is a cross street here, and through the alleyway of overgrown foliage I see a creeping figure enter the wider opening in the middle of the cracked and broken avenue.

A figure carrying an assault rifle over her arm, ready to bring it up and fire at anything that stirs.

With as little movement as possible, I reach behind my shoulder and slide an arrow from my quiver, fitting into my bow in one move. I won't fire if I don't have to, but—

Just then, I hear a rustle behind the crumbling remains of the small building behind me and freeze. I imagine myself a part of the natural world, blending into my surroundings like a rabbit beneath a fallen tree trunk.

Out of the corner of my eye, I see a flash of movement. A vine blowing in the wind? I turn my head slowly and find Sergeant Krim taking a position behind the second metal machine. He grins at me, raising a finger to his lips. Another flicker, and one of his corporals moves into place behind the third machine.

They're not supposed to be here. They're supposed to be at the finish line, waiting to welcome us into the ranks of Purple Blooded society.

Waiting to mark off the dead from their lists.

Both Krim and Corporal Aleya are armed with assault rifles, held at the ready.

I had no idea that she was on our side. I thought Krim was keeping our plan a secret. It seems he's been recruiting others to our cause, after all.

I turn back to face the street. The Purple woman is closer, trotting along lightly, swinging her own rifle from side to side, alert for any movement. I almost relax, thinking she's going to pass by, when she drops into a crouch. She scurries low to the ground and drops beneath the overgrown foliage at the edge of the street. Wriggling like a snake into a burrow, she faces the street with her rifle at the ready, extended in front of her, braced on bent elbows with her finger on the trigger.

There's not long to wait.

Spread out across the width of the street, a group of my training companions approaches stealthily, Blue Bloods and Purples together. Working together, to stay alive and make it through to the end.

Del, Ree, Kela, Piperell.

Wadyn, Dantil, Jaoan, Beva.

Xion, Geia, Raeve, and—

River.

He's still alive. Unharmed.

They don't see the woman lying concealed in the foliage, but she's seen them. She's waiting until they come even with her position and then—

Krim squeezes off a short burst of fire and she slumps over silently. The report of the rifle has alerted the approaching Sixteens, however, and they scatter, taking cover. Just in time—

The Purple woman was not alone. How could I miss that? From positions atop piles of rubble all around us, bullets begin to whiz through the air, crisscrossing the open street. Krim and Aleya begin returning fire, sighting along the tops of the crumbling buildings and behind fallen walls to fire at anything that moves.

"Wait!" I whisper hoarsely. The others...My *friends* are out there.

"Don't worry," the sarge says in a low voice, never taking his eyes off the street. "We planned this."

I glance over at Aleya to find her grinning. "This is the tightest spot on the course," she says, "coming up on the finish line. We knew they'd be waiting for you kids."

"You mean you—"

Krim allows a tiny smile to curve his lips, even as he sights and fires again, another adult falling from his perch atop a windowless three-story building. "You don't think I'd leave this all up to chance, do you?"

Aleya hasn't stopped firing either. "If this insurrection is going to succeed, we need every one of you alive and ready to fight."

It's just minutes until the returning gunfire has fallen silent, and Krim and Aleya raise their rifles.

I've stopped counting the number of bodies this Transcendent Hunt has left along the way. Choking back the bile, I follow the sarge and corporal out of our cover and into the street. Others are coming out, as well, Sixteens, some grinning, some looking sickened.

Looking around, I try to find River. He was with the others when the shooting started, but when they dove for cover, I lost sight of him. "River? Where's River?"

Sobering quickly, Dantil looks around. "He was right beside me," he says.

"I saw him duck into that doorway," one of the other girls, Geia, says, pointing across the street.

I hurry in that direction, scanning the street for any sign of further attack. At the wall of what must have once been a storefront, a floor to ceiling window blown out, I flatten myself against the bricks.

"River? River, are you here?"

No answer.

Peering around the doorjamb, I try to scan the interior. Nothing moves. I sidle inside, keeping tight to the wall, shards of broken glass crunching beneath the soles of my boots. A shadow at the rear of the empty space catches my eye. River—

But it's not River.

It's an adult. Purple Blood.

Even as he lifts his arm to fire his weapon, my arrow leaves the crossbow, zinging through the still, dusty air to take him in the throat. The body flies backwards, pinned into a wooden rack with faded lettering.

The man gurgles, blood filling his throat as he struggles weakly, trying to free himself. But in moments he is gone.

Dead on his feet.

“Ryn—”

Against a fallen display case, lying on his back in the dim space, I finally spot River and rush to his side.

He’s not getting up.

Why doesn’t he get up?

“Ryn, I—”

I kneel beside him, reaching out—

“Shh. Don’t talk. It’s going to be okay.” I pull off my bag, unzip and pull out a towel.

But the growing pool of blood spreading out from beneath him tells me what I feared from the beginning of this entire monstrous lottery. I can't lose him.

"Ryn...I'm sorry," River gasps, clawing at his middle. In the growing darkness of the ruined shop, I can see what looks like a mass of snakes, or whitish worms, falling from his abdomen. I won't be able to fix this.

River has been gutted like an animal.

Gutted, and left to die alone.

"I...always...lov—"

But he passes out then, the word left unfinished.

"Kairyn, come on!" Sergeant Krim grabs my arm, turning me around to face him, his voice low. "I've tagged his position. The medics will be here in a few minutes to retrieve him. He'll get the help he needs. But we need to move."

I can't bear it. I can't just leave River here, in the dust of this ruined building. Not when I know what he was about to say when he passed out.

I never felt the way he did. Even if I had stayed in Eie, we wouldn't have been together.

But if my blood had not tested Lorem Sanguis, at least River would never have entered the Lottery. Never joined the Hunt.

He would still be alive, safe at home.

This evil has to end.

"Kairyn, come on." I hear Sergeant Krim's stern voice behind me and turn toward the rectangle of light in the growing dusk. Behind him, crowded outside the door frame, I see the others, waiting.

Waiting to move on to the end.

Waiting to finish this Hunt.

Waiting to change Elleon forever.

"The medics will come for him, Kai," Krim says again. "But we need to move now."

I smooth back the hair from River's face, so pale in the growing dusk. So much lies between us, and so little. My friend, my confidante. We spent so many years playing in the woods, swimming in the creeks, sleeping outside under the stars. I never dreamed that River loved me the way he did. I never dreamed that he would sacrifice his safety, risk his life, to be here with me.

"I'm sorry," I say softly. "I'm sorry I wasn't who you expected me to be. I'm sorry we couldn't live the life you wanted for us. I'm sorry—"

It isn't enough. It could never be enough.

But it is all I can spare for now. For now, the lives of all the other Sixteens hang by a thread. I have obligations to fulfill.

"I will fix this," I say, rising to my feet. When I reach the doorway, I take the time to spare one last glance for my friend. "I will stop this from happening to anyone else."

In the dimming of the day, I can barely make out the forms of my teammates hidden among the fallen walls and overgrown foliage. Shadows shift as I move into the open. Sergeant Krim is beside me in an instant.

"Let's move, Kairyn."

"How many—?"

Krim reaches out to lay a hand on my shoulder. "More than I ever expected. More than ever before, in the history of the Hunt. We've done something amazing today."

Amazing.

But it's just a start.

The last mile everyone is on high alert. The slightest crackle of a fallen leaf and our weapons aim at a mouse or a bird, anything that moves. Just beyond the circle of light cast by the portable lamps set up outside the crumbled building signposted Visitor Center, Krim signals us all to drop to a crouch.

"Our being with you, helping you," he says, indicating Corporal Aleya and himself, "is a violation of the Hunt rules. It's treason. So, we have to sneak back in alone. Count to fifty to give us time to get in place, then come in by ones and twos. Not all at once. You're still a target."

In the end, there is no attack as we trickle into the cleared space. It seems like a letdown at first, two, then four, five, six of the Sixteens reaching the finish line. One or two adult Hunters are already there, getting their wounds bandaged. But as our numbers grow—more groups who came from different directions adding to our numbers—consternation begins to show on the faces of the Hunt organizers.

When I appear silently in front of the organizer's tent, filled with screens recording stats and survivors, the hushed voices conferring over the unexpected results fall silent. At the back of the tent, I see Sergeant Krim and Corporal Aleya, fighting to hide their pleased expressions. I step up to a man holding a small screen in his hands and drop my pack on the ground at his feet.

"Kairyn, from Eie," I announce. "Purple."

No one has claimed the bounty on my head.

The man's mouth twists as he checks off my name. "Congratulations," he says.

He doesn't mean it.

I make way for the next Sixteens in line, following the directions of a woman in fatigues who waves me farther into the small bastion of civilization set up in the wilderness. When our numbers reach twenty, then thirty, the military personnel and Hunt organizers begin to confer in low voices while us Sixteens group under a big tent, helping ourselves to an array of food and drinks laid out on long tables. Provisions they no doubt thought would go to the Hunters.

Hunters who began this day believing that they would walk away with some measure of fame for killing Sixteens, and a hefty prize to swell their bank accounts.

In the end, out of forty-seven of us who started this Hunt, thirty-eight of us have survived. When I check the board to see our scores, my blood freezes.

River is listed among the dead. That can't be. Sergeant Krim assured me that the medics would get to him in time. He was wrong. My friend is gone.

Did they not help him because he was Blue? Maybe this was the plan all along.

Oh, River. Why couldn't you just stay in Eie. I have to find a way back home. I need to tell his poor mom... brothers... that his death will not be in vain. I will not let this go. I'm royalty by blood. If someone is to stop this madness, it will be me.

Krim finally allows his pleasure at the results to show on his face when he joins us in the larger tent. He doesn't seem to realize that my best friend is dead. Grinning, he holds up his hands to quell the shouts of congratulations my companions are unable to hold in any longer.

I have to fight back tears. There is nothing for me to celebrate, after all.

"You've made me very proud today, recruits," he says, lifting a bottle of ale into the air in salute. "No Hunt has ever boasted such a large number of survivors. Your skills and training, and your ability to work together, has done something no other year's Sixteens has ever been able to do. The awards ceremony tomorrow will be something to see!" He raises his bottle and takes a hug swig. "For now, we need to get back to the barracks and get cleaned up. Dinner in the mess at eight!"

In the end, out of one hundred Hunters who won the Lottery, less than half made it back to Mag City. Alive and well, that is. The remainder were flown out in ambulance choppers or trucked out in body bags, along with nine Sixteens who lost their lives.

Krim is right.

No other year's Sixteens have ever done what we did.

All I can think as we fly back in the military choppers is that River isn't with me.

It is my fault that he entered the Lottery in the first place.

It is my fault that he is dead.

Chapter Eighteen

"I JUST DON'T SEE how any of this can matter, in the long run," I say. Sergeant Krim and I are sitting beside a tiny stream that runs along the rear of the complex of military buildings and barracks after returning to Mag City. "Yes, we 'won,' for what it's worth. We're still alive...most of us. But how are we supposed to change anything, really?"

I should have been asleep hours ago, exhausted by the Hunt and the grief of losing River. Somehow, though, I couldn't lie still. Krim must have seen me sneaking out of the barracks and followed me into the night to talk.

"Of course, it won't be easy," the sarge says. He's sitting beside me on the bank of the stream, elbows on his knees. "There are a lot more people in Elleon who aren't happy with the way things are, though. Both military personnel and civilians. More than I ever thought possible. We may need to move slowly, but change will happen, from the ground up."

I give an unbecoming snort. "I can't imagine King Ilan and Queen Helena just stepping down and handing over the reins of government to us. Or any of those generals and politicians who have gained wealth and power through controlling our lives."

"I'll admit, most of those congratulating me on this year's training regimen, and how superior all of you Sixteens turned out to be because of it, were lower level personnel. Not officers, granted, but among the enlisted ranks we have a lot of support. Everybody from Sergeant Majors to corporals down to privates."

Aside from Corporal Aleya, I haven't seen any sign of support. But then, would higher ups in the military risk their careers by revealing their true sympathies to a newly-created Purple Blood?

Or someone they believe to be Purple.

"The people need to know you exist. Tomorrow, when King Ilan offers the royal favor you announce that you are their daughter."

I need to remember that no one except Krim and Oma, and that doctor who did the Testing back in Eie, even know that I am *Lorem Sanguis*.

That is the reason why all this is happening, after all. If not for my royal blood, Krim might never have started his subversive plans for overthrowing the entire blood hierarchy system our country was founded on. Once the others know...

"So, at the awards ceremony tomorrow," I say slowly, "I am supposed to reveal myself to King Ilan. Why wouldn't he just order me executed then and there?"

"Timing is everything," Krim says. "Even he has to behave honorably, in public at least. As of today, you are one of Elleon's elite. When he calls you up to the podium to bestow your award for the highest bounties collected and the greatest number of enemies killed or disabled, he is honor-bound to allow you to ask for a favor. That's when you announce who you are, and what you want. He won't be able to refuse."

Krim and I had discuss this plan in depth. On the podium, I was supposed to announce that I was Crown Prince Hern's twin sister. King Ilan and Queen Helena's long-lost daughter. They may have tried to remove me as an infant, but now, as a highly trained and blood-proven member of the royal family, I should be fairly safe from assassination.

I was also going to demand that Sergeant Krim be assigned as my personal bodyguard. He just didn't know it yet.

After several long moments of silence, I turn to him, the outline of his sharp features barely visible in the light of the waning moon. I feel an unfamiliar affection for this man who has protected me, guided me, trained me. Who has, after all, saved my life through his cunning.

"Thank you," I say, and lean in to kiss his cheek.

But I have surprised him. He whips his head around to face me. Our lips meet and we both jump back, shocked. I never meant to kiss him like that.

It was supposed to be a peck on the cheek. A kiss for a big brother. For a friend.

But his lips felt so right. I lean forward again, ever so slightly.

This isn't River. Isn't just a friend.

I want to taste his lips again.

And he seems to feel the same as I do. Sergeant Krim. Xandyr Krim.

Xandyr.

This is the first time I've allowed myself to think of him by his first name. I like the way it feels in my mind. "Xandyr," I say, and I like the feel of his name on my tongue, in my mouth...

He leans in then and our lips meet again, not by accident. By design.

Several long minutes pass as we explore each other's lips, as our hands seek and find shoulders, pulling us closer together. Run the length of each other's spines, arching inward to bring ourselves into the other. Press our legs together, rubbing thighs and calves and boots. If we weren't in fatigues right now—

If we weren't fatigued right now...

But this is not how I want to know him. Xandyr Krim. Not rolling around on the muddy stream bank. Not with muscles already strained from the day's exertions.

And I know he feels the same when he pulls away, looking down at me with eyes that reflect the pale moonlight. I smile slightly, sigh.

"After tomorrow—"

Xandyr smiles back. "After tomorrow," he agrees.

Chapter Nineteen

THE STADIUM IS HUNG with banners and streamers when we march in, our formation tight, precise. We are all proud of what we have accomplished, and it shows in our military bearing.

There is not nearly the level of noise, of cheering, as on the first day we entered this place, the day of the Transcendent Lottery. The adults of Mag City do not cheer so enthusiastically or wave their little flags so much.

Forty-seven newly Tested Sixteens have upset their beliefs, destroyed their image of themselves as superior in all ways.

My chin lifts a little higher. They have no idea how much their lives are about to change.

My eyes seek out King Ilan and Queen Helena on the stage set at the end of the field. Their gold-painted throne-like chairs rest in the center of the stage, raised above the seats of the officials who surround them. In a smaller chair beside them sits my brother, Prince Hern. After today, they'll need to order another golden chair for me.

Princess Kairyn.

Sergeant Krim's Sixteens remain in our formation as we take the field, standing at attention facing the stage. The sweat begins to run down our faces as we stand there in the hot sun, but not one of us reaches up to wipe a forehead. We are military now.

The speeches start.

Government officials announce awards of merit, handing out medals.

And when all of that is done, King Ilan and Queen Helena rise and walk to the microphone.

King Ilan looks even more grim and stony-faced than usual. Queen Helena blinks rapidly, as if she is holding back tears. When the king takes the microphone in his hand, Queen Helena steps back, leaving him to speak.

"People of Elleon," he begins, "this is a solemn day for our nation."

There is a stirring among the crowds in the stands. I stand beside Sergeant Krim, the highest ranked in our squad after the Hunt. I can feel the sudden tightness in his stance. What is going on?

"People of Elleon," King Ilan says again, "I know that you—like Queen Helena and I—are disappointed in the results of yesterday's Transcendent Hunt. Many of Elleon's finest Hunters, the elite of our society, were injured or killed. This is unprecedented in the many years which our most sacred tradition has stood as a gateway into our ranks."

He pauses for a moment, as if he, too, is swallowing back tears.

But I am standing just below the stage, barely feet away from our ruler. And I can see that he is not saddened, not by a long shot.

He is furious.

King Ilan's eyes dip to the ranked Sixteens on the field. Those cold eyes pass over the rows of Purples and Blues below him until they stop on me. Meet my eyes. Stop. Hold.

I feel them burning into me like the laser sight on a rifle.

My father's eyes.

"While we are proud of the showing of our young people, under the direction and training of one of Elleon's elite soldiers, Sergeant Xandyr Krim," he says, "it is the finding of the medical corps that our Hunters were compromised prior to the competition!"

The uproar is instantaneous. Throughout the stadium the crowds rise to their feet screaming for blood. King Ilan's lips quirk upwards in a near-smile, but he quickly regains his grim look.

I think back to everything we did that night. Did we leave something that gave us away?

“Now, now,” he says, signaling with his hands for the viewers to take their seats again. “We are investigating this sabotage. My elite officers will get to the bottom of this very quickly.”

Is he saying that we somehow drugged our opponents to gain an advantage? Or that we poisoned them? That is ridiculous!

Our advantage was simply working together to defeat a better armed and better trained enemy.

“It is the preliminary finding of our intelligence officers that the sabotage was a Red Blood plot to bring down our government. As you know, the rebellion has gained strength in recent months. We are even now deploying troops to the border areas where these scum hide to plot our downfall. The Red Bloods will be quickly rooted out and put to death, to the last man and woman.”

My jaw tightens. Sweat is dripping down my face but I can’t break formation to wipe it away. I fear that if I move a muscle, I won’t be able to control myself. I will leap from the ground of the field to the top of the stage and wrap my hands around his throat.

All this time, I have believed—like everyone else—that the Red Blood rebels were our enemy. But now I can see that they are just another convenient fiction to keep us all under control. The king is blaming the Reds for our victory in the Transcendent Hunt, to give him another excuse to tighten his hold over everyone in Elleon.

"In the meantime," King Ilan goes on, "we have been forced to discard the results of yesterday's Transcendent Hunt."

At this, the Sixteens lose their military bearing. We all burst out in yells of outrage. All of our efforts to overturn this rigged system have been thrown away in mere seconds. Xandyr quickly swings around and quells our shouts with a slash of his arm through the air. That and a harsh look. Even now, he demands adherence to military protocol.

We snap to attention once more, eyes forward. But standing at the sergeant's side, I can feel burning waves of seething anger rolling off of my comrades in arms.

"It would be unfair to the people of Elleon," the king says, "to honor the results of a compromised Hunt. The bounties on all participants have been withdrawn and the funds pledged returned to all bettors. In addition, the traditional favor granted to the highest scoring among the Sixteens is also withdrawn."

It feels as if the ground is crumbling out from beneath my feet.

That favor was my chance to claim my birthright. To join the royal family and take my place as Princess Kairyn. To reveal myself to the mother who gave me up rather than see me put to death for the crime of being born a twin.

That favor was my chance to overturn the entire corrupt system of governance in Elleon, and create a society based not on blood, but on human value.

And it has been stripped away. Ripped away.

It is too much.

"You can't do this!" I shout. Krim swings around and grabs my arm, but I fight to shake him off. I will not be silenced.

With a huge running leap, I jump onto the stage. The guards race from the edges of the stage, but there are too many officials in the way for them to reach me easily. I grab the microphone as the king steps back, his hand on his ceremonial sword.

Our eyes meet. Lock.

This is no father of mine. He is an accident of blood.

"You cannot deny us our rights!" I shout into the microphone so that everyone in the stadium, everyone watching the ceremony on screens placed in the many communities across the country, can hear. “We have earned our reward! You dishonor the crown of Elleon!”

The guards reach my side at last. I am without a weapon to defend myself, so I pick up the microphone stand in my hands and swing it like a staff. I connect with one man’s head, catching another full across the chest as I swing the stand back again. But there are too many of them. They wrestle the stand from my hands. Yank my arms behind my back.

I have just one chance.

“I am your daughter!” I scream as they lead me away. “I am Princess Kairyn, sister of Prince Hern! I am of royal blood!”

I think that no one has heard my outcry in the midst of the pandemonium. Below the stage, the Sixteens are being surrounded by more guards, and herded toward the exit gate. Xandyr is with them, but is he detaining his Sixteens, or being detained? It’s impossible to tell as the guards cuff my hands behind my back.

My eyes catch those of Queen Helena, and I see the truth. She knows me.

“I am your daughter,” I shout again, praying for her to intercede.

But she doesn’t move. Doesn’t speak.

Doesn't acknowledge me.

One of the guards lifts his baton then, and with one blow to my head, everything goes black.

Chapter Twenty

WHEN I COME TO, I find myself lying on a concrete floor surrounded by the Sixteens. I struggle upwards, pulling my legs beneath me, my head pounding as I kneel upright. My hands are still cuffed behind my back.

Everyone is handcuffed and kneeling, but the others' hands are restrained in front of them.

I alone am deemed dangerous enough to have my arms pulled painfully behind my back.

Around me in the large, dim room I hear sniffles and groans, but at least no one has lost total control. There is no one crying. No one screaming. They at least maintain that small measure of control.

"Where...where are we?" I ask, looking around. I don't recognize this place.

Are we in prison?

Jeaol is on one side of me, Radyn the other, with her brother Wadyn propped against her bent shoulders. Wadyn's face is bloody. His sister has been wiping the blood out of his eyes with the sleeve of her uniform.

It is Jeaol who answers my question.

"Storage area," he says brusquely. "Beneath the stadium."

"What are they—"

"No idea." Jeaol doesn't seem to want to talk.

Radyn turns to me, shifting on her knees. "Are you all right, Kai?" she asks. "When we saw you jump onto the stage, we thought they'd kill you!"

"I'm okay," I say. "Got hit on the head—"

I can feel the blood trickling down from my temple. Unlike Wadyn, I don't have a sister to wipe it away.

I do have a brother, but—

With a gasp, I drop my head forward.

I have a brother who shares my blood. Lorem Sanguis. My blood is Lorem Sanguis. Everyone who sees me bleeding will know instantly that I spoke the truth when I tried to reveal my origins.

I shouldn't have tried. My timing was definitely off. But maybe no one heard me or discounted my claim.

At this point, it might be more dangerous than helpful. After all, my father would have killed me before, when I was born. What's to stop him from killing me now? There is no audience of Elleon's citizens to bear witness. No one to protest my killing. No one except the other Sixteens, clustered around me in handcuffs. Prisoners, like me.

King Ilan would, I have no doubt now, kill all of them to hide what I am.

Sudden noise at the far end of the room signals the arrival of more guards. The scarred metal doors swing open, and they march in, Sergeant Krim among them. I heave a sigh of relief. I didn't realize how worried I was about Xandyr, only realizing now that I see him that he, too, could have been imprisoned with us.

They don't know how much he was a part of our act of rebellion.

Thank the gods for small favors!

Behind the guards, surprisingly, King Ilan, Queen Helena, and Prince Hern enter the vast storage room. Xandyr steps forward and speaks with the king in a low voice, then turns to face us.

“Eyes forward!” he orders.

Everyone snaps to attention, as well as we are able to with our hands cuffed. Slowly, the royals stalk down the line of Sixteens, King Ilan stopping to look each of us over thoroughly. Sergeant Krim follows Prince Hern. At least it appears that no one has determined his involvement. His cover is intact.

Good news. As long as no one knows he was a part of our plan to win the Hunt, he is safe from punishment.

The king is angry, very angry. I can tell from the set of his face, from the flush in his cheeks. From the stiff way he walks. He is unyielding.

When he reaches me, near the end of the line, he stops. Stands. Looks.

My hair falls over my forehead, hiding the trickle of blood which runs down from the split above my forehead.

Suddenly King Ilan’s hand whips out and slaps me full across the face. I can feel the welts his broad fingers leave rising across my cheek. My jaw stiffens as I fight to control myself, fight to remain on my knees before him.

Out of the corner of my eye, I see Sergeant Krim start forward, as if he will punch the king. He can't. He mustn't! Luckily, the guard behind him grabs his arm and pulls him back into line. Xandyr struggles with the woman, but she whispers one sharp word in his ear and he goes still. Steps back into line. Though Prince Hern is closest to him and had to notice the scuffle, he doesn't react.

My brother has perfect control.

I could learn from him.

If I ever get the chance to know him.

But I've judged the situation too soon. King Ilan turns slowly to face Krim as Queen Helena and Prince Hern move aside to allow the king a clear view of our commanding officer. "Sergeant, step forward," King Ilan says sharply.

Out of the corner of my eye I watch Xandyr march briskly to a position directly in front of the king, snapping his heels together and giving a brisk salute. The silence in the echoing room is total for several moments before the king speaks again.

"Sergeant Krim," King Ilan says, "we have heard disturbing rumors of an inappropriate relationship between you and this recruit. In fact, you were witnessed kissing the recruit on the grounds of the training complex, after the Hunt. I, myself, have observed an unwarrantedly friendly attitude between the two of you, while watching the training footage. Please explain yourself."

"Sir, I have done nothing wrong, sir!"

"Are you denying the eyewitness account of the officer who say you wrapped around this recruit in a passionate embrace?"

"Sir, no, sir!" Xandyr looks green. He knows how dangerous it would be to admit to an inappropriate relationship with a subordinate. "Our relationship as training officer and recruit ended when the Hunt ended. There was nothing inappropriate, sir!"

"And we are to believe that nothing...*untoward* happened between the two of you during the long weeks of training?"

"That is correct, sir. Nothing happened between us before that time."

"Hmmm," the king turns away, looking down at my bent head where I kneel on the ground beside my fellow Sixteens. "Perhaps nothing *happened*, but that doesn't mean that your personal feelings didn't lead you to commit treason by subverting the goals of the Transcendent Hunt, our most sacred tradition. Your allegiance to Elleon and to your military command, I believe, have been compromised by your lust for this outer community slut!"

Xandyr is silent, his jaw clenched on the sharp words he doesn't dare speak in the face of the king. But King Ilan isn't finished yet.

"In fact," he goes on, "I believe that you have knowingly subverted the goals of Elleon by using unorthodox training methods with this year's Sixteens, in order to allow your *inamorata* to win. No other year's Sixteens have performed so subversively, with so many of them making it through the Hunt alive, to claim the hard-earned bounties placed on their heads. You are a traitor to Elleon and to your king!"

The silence in the room is complete. No one so much as breathes.

I want to scream a denial, but I catch Xandyr's eyes on me. He shakes his head briefly, barely a twitch. I hold my protest inside.

"Guards, arrest this man!" the king commands, and they move forward to grasp Krim's arms on either side, restraining him in place. "Take him to the White Hall."

Everyone in Elleon knows that the White Hall, the impenetrable fortress where the worst criminals in the nation are held until convicted—and all are convicted once accused—is inescapable. Confinement in the White Hall is a death sentence.

"No!" I stumble to my feet, my arms behind my back. "No! Don't! It was my fault! I am the one who planned it all! You can't blame Xandyr—"

King Ilan swings around to face me directly. He glares at me for a long second, then raises his hand again.

Crack!

The backhanded blow knocks me back to my knees on the concrete floor. His royal signet ring has scored a deep gash across my cheek, tearing open my flesh. The pain is excruciating, but I clamp my lips shut, refusing to cry out.

“Take her to the White Hall, as well!” King Ilan roars, turning away as more guards rush forward and drag me back to my feet.

The woman clutching my right arm, holding me upright, gasps. She steps back, allowing everyone in the room a clear view of my face. The king swings back around to see what everyone is looking at, even as Queen Helena moves forward. King Ilan blocks her with an outstretched arm, but she clutches his wrist as she points at my face.

Murmurs rise throughout the room. Even in the dim light, I know what everyone here is seeing. I feel it, in the warmth running down my face.

They see my blood. Not Purple, as it is supposed to be.

They see my royal blood.

Lorem Sanguis.

Purple, Blue, and Red. All together. The sign of ultimate superiority.

“Impossible!” King Ilan shouts, moving as fast as a snake to strike me again. But Queen Helena grabs his arm, pulling it down and holding it tightly. He turns to look down into her tear-streaked face.

He sees the truth, before she even speaks the words.

“Ilan, my love,” the queen says. “It’s true. She is our daughter.”

Chapter Twenty-one

KING ILAN HAS GONE pale as death. He stares at me, *Lorem Sanguis* blood running from the wound his blow has left on my cheek. The room is completely silent now, no one daring to breathe.

"How...how is this..." the king struggles to find the simple words in his shocked state. "*Possible*?"

"During my pregnancy, I was afraid there was something... different. Unusual. When the child was finally born, and was a girl, I knew there could be a conflict of succession. A girl has never assumed the throne of Elleon. But over the last hundred years, many have begun to question our laws of primogeniture. 'Why shouldn't there be a female ruler,' they ask." She takes a deep breath and pulls her shoulders back. "I, myself, have asked that question."

Uncomfortable rustlings sound throughout the dim space, echoing off the concrete floor. Prince Hern—my brother—steps forward and rests a hand on the queen's shoulder. He is on his mother's side.

Perhaps he doesn't care so much for being the next ruler of Elleon.

He glances my way briefly, and I would swear that I see...what? His eyes seem warm, seeking...connection? Is he pleased to discover that he has a sister?

"But then," Queen Helena goes on, "my labor continued. The pangs of childbirth grew strong again, and the midwife sent everyone out of the room. They didn't need to be there for the afterbirth, she said. When Hern was born a few minutes later, we knew that the girl—our firstborn—was in danger of her life. I sent the midwife to summon Colonel Krim," she glances aside at Xandyr, Sergeant Krim, the son of the man who spirited me away as an infant and took me to Eie to be fostered by Oma. "Colonel Krim took the child out of the palace before anyone could know of her existence. He took her somewhere safe. Somewhere even I didn't know about."

She turns from the king and steps across the concrete floor to stand in front of me. "This is our daughter, Ilan." She reaches out with a shaking hand to brush back the hair from my forehead, the gesture of a mother who cares even when she doesn't know her child. She stares deep into my eyes for a long moment before turning back to the king.

"I knew that you would put our daughter to death, to secure the throne for your son," she says. "I couldn't allow that to happen."

The king's jaw tightens as he stares at his traitorous wife. "You have endangered our entire nation by your sympathetic foolishness," he says harshly. "You have endangered our only son's inheritance. I could have you executed for your act of treason. You and this...*thing*, both!"

He turns away, taking in the silent audience of guards and Sixteens both. He suddenly realizes that everyone here is a threat to him now. We have all seen him at his weakest, betrayed by the queen's act of mercy.

What will he do now?

Will he have everyone in this room executed to protect his throne?

"Guards, take these abominations back to the barracks," he orders, waving a negligent hand in the direction of the line of Sixteens, kneeling before him on the concrete with their hands cuffed in front of them.

The guards look uncomfortable, glancing aside at one another as they rouse the kneeling recruits to their feet. I wonder if they realize that their lifespan has just been cut short.

And that it is my fault.

How could we have ever thought that attempting to claim my place in the royal family would work?

"Tomorrow," the king goes on, "I will announce a second Hunt, to right the wrongs of this year's failed Transcendent Hunt. The Hunt which was compromised by the perfidious actions of Sergeant Krim and this one girl. The results cannot be allowed to stand."

He pauses to gather his thoughts.

"It is obvious to us that Sergeant Krim's lust for this recruit, and her lack of self-control, have led to them corrupting the entire class of recruits. For this reason, we think it is only fair that a second competition be initiated. We must still allow this year's Sixteens—who are blameless in all of this—the chance to earn their rightful place in Elleon's great society."

He turns to Queen Helena then, his face cold.

He shakes his head as if he is scolding an errant child.

"I am very disappointed in you, my dear," he says. Queen Helena's body is ramrod straight and it's obvious she is fighting to hold her emotions in check.

How must it feel to find the daughter you gave away Sixteen years ago is alive and standing in front of you, only to be blamed for her existence?

"Your transgression, your flaunting of our sacred laws, the very fabric of our society, cannot go unpunished. You have proven yourself unworthy of your position." He steps closer to the queen, reaching out to grasp her chin in his hand and force her face upwards. For a heartbeat he stares coldly into her eyes.

If he ever loved Helena, that love is long gone.

"As your punishment," he says slowly, clearly, "you will join your daughter in the Second Hunt. Let's see if you fight for your life —and hers—as nobly as you did on the night she was born."

Prince Hern gasps in shock at his father's cruelty.

He must realize—as we all do—that a Second Hunt means death for the majority of us. And the queen is not a young woman, fit to fight for her life. His mother has just been sentenced to death.

By his father.

Queen Helena flicks her eyes to the crown prince's shocked face. Shakes her head. Warns him to silence. Then she raises her hands in front of her, wrists together.

Ready to share the shackles which bind the Sixteens.

Which bind her daughter.

Ready to fight—and die—at our sides.

My mother.

Chapter Twenty-two

I HAVEN'T SEEN XANDYR since three days ago at the awards ceremony ago, when we were all removed from the stadium under guard. I worry every minute about him, how he's being treated. I worry about what punishment he will receive when he is brought to trial.

I worry about the torture he's subject to in the White Hall prison at the hands of the guards. Men he possibly trained or served with.

How will they treat a man they believe has betrayed their nation?

The Second Hunt was announced on the screens within days, the king's decree broadcast throughout Elleon for everyone to see. We have been living under guard—and in disgrace—for ten days when we are woken early one morning and loaded into buses for the trip to a new venue, one we've never visited during our training sessions.

I thought that at least I would have this time to get to know my birth mother, Queen Helena. She was brought to the training complex with us Sixteens after the king decreed that she join us in the Second Hunt. But she has been kept under guard in a separate apartment this whole time.

When we were allowed out into the grounds for exercise, I often looked up to find her pale face at the window of her bedroom, looking back at me. But if I tried to wave or smile at her, the nearest guards would pummel me with their batons or stun me with an electrogun.

They apparently still had the respect instilled in them for the royal family, even when one of those royals was condemned to fight for her life in a Hunt.

Today, however, when they march us outside under cloud-filled skies, and load us into the buses, the guards aren't so punitive. They don't seem to care anymore if the queen is approached by a mere Sixteen. I slide into the seat beside her, looking straight ahead so that we aren't discovered talking to each other. Just in case...

"I'm so sorry—"

I keep my voice low, barely moving my lips.

Queen Helena—my mother—takes my hand in hers, hiding the movement between our bodies so that the guards don't see the personal interaction. She squeezes my fingers.

"Don't be sorry," she replies, following my lead and barely moving her lips as she whispers. "This isn't your fault."

"If I hadn't encouraged them all to work together, to defeat the Hunters—"

"The truth would have come out sooner or later," she says, "when your blood was seen by someone, anyone. A simple papercut. A pulled tooth at the dentist. It was impossible that you wouldn't be discovered, after you received the serum."

We sit in silence for most of the ride, until Queen Helena perks up, sitting taller in the seat beside me and craning her neck forward to look through the broad windshield of the bus. She looks even more worried than when we boarded the buses.

"What? What is it?" I whisper.

"I know where they're taking us," she whispers back, her forehead furrowed with deep creases. "This is the newest military training facility," she says. "The highest tech, the most deadly weapons. This will not be as easy as running through the woods or stabbing someone with a knife. There are no projectile weapons here. No guns or bows and arrows. This is a testing ground for laser weapons. Weapons that track by body heat or by scent. The AI systems are deadly accurate at anticipating an opponent's movements."

Her hand tightens on mine, crushing my fingers. She turns to look into my eyes and raises her free hand to caress my cheek as a mother does an infant in her arms.

"This isn't good."

Her words are quiet, but the guards have seen the caress. The one closest to me flies down the aisle of the bus and punches me in the ear. It doesn't matter that it was Queen Helena who touched me. They can't attack her, so I take the punishment.

The ringing in my ear lasts for several seconds. By the time I shake it off, we've pulled up in front of double metal doors set into a nondescript wall. Within minutes, we're all marched off the buses and lined up in double rows under threatening skies.

The queen is alone at the front of the column, a guard on either side.

We are marched into a darkened arena complex formed of transparent walls. The central area is round, with enclosed tunnels leading off at intervals to other transparent pods. The whole complex is enormous.

We are dwarfed by the scale of this arena.

Ants waiting to be crushed under the king's boot heel.

Slowly, one section at a time, the lights flick on throughout the vast space. Around the outer edge are holographic seats filled with Mag City residents. They are watching us from the comfort and safety of their homes.

As the lights come up throughout the arena, we see the encircling pods through the transparent walls. There are different settings in each one, as if we will be playing a video game. Playing *within* a video game.

I see a field of broken ice in one, a desert sandscape with towering sandstone monoliths in another. A dismal swamp, trees hung with dripping swags of moss. An underground cavern with narrow tunnels running through it like an ant hill. And those are the natural-appearing settings.

Others, more high-tech, are graphic representations of battlefields, with digital floors and walls that shift and reform as they float through the air. One is a maze, with constantly moving walls. Another is filled with human-sized bubbles. The bubbles have spikes sticking out on all sides, and when one bounces against another, the smaller one explodes with a bang.

We are clustered together at one side of the central round arena when a brilliant white spotlight flicks on over the center and a holographic podium appears. The podium looks like it has been carved from an enormous diamond, faceted and scintillating with refracted light. We wait, still and ready, to see what will happen next.

My fellow Sixteens have drawn away to one side, leaving me alone with the queen. They look away when I glance their way, trying to offer a smile, a show of solidarity and support.

No one smiles back.

They all look extremely uncomfortable. I guess our "one for all" ploy from the Transcendent Hunt has evaporated. This time, it's going to be everyone for themselves.

They can play it that way if they like. I will protect my birth mother to the best of my ability, and myself, as well. I won't abandon her.

Within moments, applause rises from the audience in the holographic seats around the outer walls, and King Ilan and Prince Hern appear on the podium, dressed in quasi-military uniforms hung with medals and braids.

My brother stands a step behind our father. He looks uncomfortable, his eyes flicking from side to side, even though his body is completely still. Contained. He gives nothing away of his emotions, although he must be horrified at the sight of his always-elegant mother standing below the podium in the arena, dressed in military fatigues and combat boots.

King Ilan holds up his hands in greeting, as well as to quiet the cheers that arose at his arrival. Within seconds, complete silence falls over the arena.

"People of Elleon, welcome to this very special event, the first-ever Second Hunt!" King Ilan's face is drawn and gray. He hasn't taken the news of my existence—or of Queen Helena's concealing the birth of her twins—well. His voice drops into a lower register. "We regret sincerely that this Second Hunt has proven necessary. But we see no other way for this year's Sixteens to fairly earn their place amongst us, after the treachery which betrayed them all in the traditional Transcendent Hunt."

He pauses, looking saddened by his memories.

He's quite an actor.

"As well, this year's Second Hunt will serve as punishment for those who undermined the spirit and the rules of the Transcendent Hunt. No one wants to see those transgressors go unpunished. We thought long and hard about the best way to deal with these traitors."

Long and hard? We were held in that concrete storeroom for maybe an hour before the king came down to tell us what our punishment would be.

If revenge is a dish best served cold, then King Ilan must have flash-frozen this retribution.

"I know that we are all feeling betrayed by the perfidious actions of Sergeant Xandyr Krim, who was entrusted with the sacred duty of training this year's Sixteens for the annual Transcendent

Hunt. He betrayed the trust placed in him by this entire nation when he conspired with one of his pupils to bypass the norms of the competition. A pupil, I might add, with whom he had an illicit relationship!"

All around the arena shouts of outrage rise, shaking the walls. I know that it's just an effect of the sound system, amplifying the sound to bone-jarring levels. But the uproar hits me on a very personal level.

That pupil Sergeant Krim conspired with is me. And although that "illicit relationship" was nothing more than a few kisses at the end of our training, I feel ashamed.

If not for me, Xandyr would not be imprisoned right now, awaiting who knows what kind of fate. He will certainly be stripped of his military rank, at the very least. At worst, he faces execution. But there is no way to know yet what his fate will be. Charges haven't yet been filed.

Whatever happens, it will be my fault.

"But Sergeant Krim trained these Sixteens and trained them too well. We feel it is only right that he rejoins his squad temporarily."

And down one of the tunnels a battered figure emerges into the arena. Xandyr's fatigues are ripped and filthy, his face bruised and bloodied. He holds his left arm tight to his body, the fingers of that hand twisted. They've broken his fingers already. The gods only know what torture awaits him.

If he survives this day.

If any of us survive this day.

I can't worry about that now, though. Standing here in this arena, surrounded by the other Sixteens, I can't allow my attention to be divided. I need to focus on the coming Second Hunt. A Hunt for which we have received no further training in the ten days since King Ilan told us of our fate.

We have no idea what is coming at us here. No idea how to win. How to survive.

We're going to need to rely on instinct, and on the training Krim provided for the first Hunt.

"Sergeant Krim was immediately arrested and imprisoned, awaiting his punishment," King Ilan addresses the people of Elleon. "Today, we need to right the wrongs he inflicted upon our entire nation. I have thought much on this, and in consultation with my most trusted advisors, have determined that we will allow the young recruits he betrayed to be the instrument of his punishment. At the same time these brave young Sixteens," he waves his hand, indicating us standing on the arena floor below him, "have the chance to compete for their place in our society, just as the Sixteens of every year since

Elleon's founding have done. Just as you, yourselves, have had the opportunity to do!"

Deafening cheers shake the walls again.

The people of Elleon are completely taken in by their king's noble words.

Of course they are taken in.

This is exactly how they, and their parents before them, have maintained the status quo. By fighting for the scraps of status and wealth that are given to them.

But King Ilan isn't finished yet.

"As well, the girl who stoked Sergeant Krim's lust and led him to betray his position as a military officer will also face retribution in this Second Hunt." A pair of guards move forward from the sidelines and grab my arms, forcing me across the floor of the arena to stand beside Xandyr.

He grins at me through the streaks of blood on his face. "Be you, Kai. Fearless," he says. At his words, one of the guards standing behind him raises his baton and brings it down on the back of Xandyr's head. There's a roar of approval from the holographic audience when he falls to his knees.

It takes him a long moment to struggle to his feet again. The guards holding me immobile tighten their grip on my arms, as if they're afraid I'll try to help him up.

They're right.

I would help him, if I could.

I look over at the other Sixteens to see what their reaction is. Not what I expected of my fellow recruits, who all these many weeks seemed loyal to their commanding officer. Their faces are hardened, set in grim lines.

Sergeant Krim and I are now their enemies.

"Now, I am afraid that I must share another piece of very distressing news with you, my people." The king pauses, wiping away a fake tear. "As a result of Sergeant Krim's arrest, we learned that the betrayal of the very fabric of our society, of its sacred laws, was subverted by the perfidious actions Sixteen years ago by my own beloved wife, Queen Helena."

Complete silence falls over the holographic seats around the perimeter of the arena.

Shocked silence, just as King Ilan intended.

"As you know, the birth of twins in the royal family would lead to challenges to the succession. If a royal couple brings twin boys into this world, then the older—even by a minute or two—becomes the heir to the throne. There is no place in our laws for the existence of a twin, and the very existence of a challenger to the heir could lead to a fight for the throne and the murder of the true heir, thereby usurping the succession."

Twins have only been born to the king and queen twice before in our history. Elleon is a young nation, born of the conflict of the Blood War.

"Queen Helena bore twins in secret," King Ilan's voice rises, outraged. Gasps can be heard from around the arena. "The legitimate heir to my throne stands beside me!" He pulls Prince Hern forward by his shoulder. My brother looks uncomfortable, but he doesn't resist. "Queen Helena, in an attempt to subvert the laws of Elleon, hid the second twin, sending it away to be fostered in secret, so that that twin could one day challenge the true heir for my throne. That second twin is the slut who seduced Sergeant Krim into betraying his people and his nation. These three conspired to destroy the Elleon we all hold dear!"

More guards now surround Queen Helena. They don't lay their hands on her, but their proximity forces her into motion, moving to join Xandyr and me.

In a flash, the spotlight focused on the king and his heir splits, half of it lighting us up where we stand in fatigues on the floor below. Sergeant Krim. Queen Helena. And me.

“There you have it, my people!” the king’s voice rises triumphantly. “Queen Helena and her illegitimate daughter! Well, I will not allow the selfish actions of your former queen to endanger this nation! As just punishment for her betrayal, Helena will join her daughter in the arena, to fight for that daughter’s life, and for her own!”

One of the guards pulls a can of spray paint from his vest. Steps in front of Xandyr, then me, then my birth mother. Sprays a huge red X across our fatigues, marking us as the targets.

The cheers are truly deafening this time, rising in a bloodlust roar that grows and grows.

Beneath the roar, words begin to emerge in an audible chant.

“Death to Queen Helena!”

“Death to the usurper!”

“Death to the Blues!”

It’s fully ten minutes before the shouts begin to die away, as the crowd vents it’s bloodlust.

“In this Second Hunt, anything goes. The Sixteens will hunt each other, yes. But the highest points—and bounties—will be awarded for the deaths of these three enemies of the state.”

Another huge board lights up behind the podium, displaying a rankings area on one side, with each of our names listed. Queen Helena's name is at the very top. On the other side is another list of our names with the bounties placed on our heads. Again, Queen Helena's is at the top, with an astronomical figure placed on her head. I am immediately after, with Xandyr just below me.

Anyone who kills any of the three of us will be set for life.

"Weapons are secreted around the arena for the contestants to defend themselves. And so, without further delay," King Ilan says, pointing to a huge digital clock suspended behind the podium, "start the clock."

Foot-high numbers light up on the black board.

00:00:30.

In thirty seconds the Second Hunt begins.

00:00:20.

Fear is written on the faces of my fellow recruits, but also determination.

00:00:10.

We search the area around us, looking for signs of weapons secreted nearby.

00:00:03.

00:00:02.

00:00:01.

00:00:00.

We run. Looking everywhere for weapons. Pulling laser pistols from behind rocks. Digging through sand to uncover blaster rifles. Climbing trees to unhook electric swords.

And the Second Hunt begins.

Chapter Twenty-three

"RUN, YOUR MAJESTY!"

At my shout, my birth mother takes off, racing for a blast gun she's spotted among the holographic rocks lining one of the tunnels. I see her grab it from the hiding place without slowing, swinging it to her shoulder as she disappears into the desert environment of the pod at the end of the tunnel.

I turn to Xandyr, but he shakes his head. He plants a hand in the small of my back, pushing me in the direction Queen Helena has taken. It's the only way I can go.

There's no time to think.

I take off after the queen. After my mother.

She saved my life on the day I was born. Now, I will save hers, or die trying.

I need to find a weapon. My boots pound the ground as I fly down the tunnel into the desert setting. Sand flies up as I climb a towering dune, following my mother's boot prints uphill.

I trip in the shifting sand as something catches my boot. Scrabbling around near my feet, I grasp the stock of a laser rifle at the same time as I leap upright, swinging the rifle from side to side. No one else is in sight yet. I take off again without further delay.

Sweat is dripping down my face by the time I reach the top of the dune. My mother is nowhere in sight. I look around quickly, trying to orient myself, but a wave of dizziness washes over me.

When I look back down the dune the way I've come, I see Xandyr about twenty feet behind, following me uphill, a plasma pistol in each hand. Good. He's armed. When I look ahead, I see the entrance to another tunnel at ground level.

The dune is an optical illusion.

We're still on flat ground, despite the exertion of the climb through the shifting sand.

This specially built training environment messes with all of my senses, making me believe that what I see is real when it's far from it. I need to try to keep that in mind.

This entire AI environment is an illusion, meant to disorient trainees.

Now I see why the sarge insisted on us recruits training with the virtual reality devices alongside our regular firearms, martial arts, and other skills. Although they weren't useful in the field for the Transcendent Hunt, they will be necessary here.

Luckily, I was pretty good with them.

With Xandyr close behind, I head for the tunnel entrance. Queen Helena is nowhere in sight. I need to catch up with her.

I need to protect her.

I have no idea what her level of skill will be, and she's in danger. Every Sixteen-year-old has to take part in the Transcendent Hunt, along with their peers. If you're *Lorem Sanguis*, like myself and Prince Hern, participation is optional. I know that Queen Helena competed in her year. Every Purple takes part in order to gain status and cement their place in our society, while only a few Blues choose to leave their home communities behind and join the Hunt. So, even though Queen Helena would have competed, it has been a very long time since then.

She won't be anywhere near skilled enough to stay alive against the angry onslaught of all of this year's Sixteens. She'll need me —and Xandyr—to protect her.

He's caught up to me by the time I'm halfway through the tunnel into the next pod. We slow together, each flattening against opposite sides of the tunnel walls to peer out and see what awaits.

No sign of the queen.

But then, there's no way to see what lies more than four feet in any direction.

The virtual reality setting appears as solid as any stone wall. And on the walls, there are several big ones right in front of us, soaring into the sky.

It appears to be a ruined castle, the outer walls stretching off to the left and right. And the walls seem to reach far beyond the height of the actual pod walls and ceiling. Queen Helena must be somewhere in that castle ruin.

I giggle at the thought.

"What's so funny?" Xandyr moves in behind my shoulder, his pistol raised. He sights along the barrel of the gun, ready to fire on anything that moves. His features are set in a mean-looking scowl.

I giggle again at the look on his face and his scowl deepens.

"It's just..." I can't quite seem to find the words. "And now... you....you look so serious!"

“I am serious! Kai, this isn’t a game. We’re under attack!”

“Well, not exactly,” I feel my mood change like a river, going from peaceful and light to a raging torrent flowing over rapids. “No one has fired a single shot! We need to find them. Kill them. Kill them all!”

Xandyr’s eyes fill with tears suddenly and he’s bawling like a little kid. “We love them! We can’t kill them. They’re our friends.”

Through the haze of flip flopping emotions, I try to think. But my brain is so fuzzy.

I look around at the castle pod, what little I can see from the entrance. The air is hazy, foggy. Or is that just my vision, clouding over?

Shaking my head, I step back into the tunnel and lean against the rounded gray wall. Drop to my knees and breath deeply. The air is clearer here near the floor. When I look up at Xandyr I realize what’s happening.

I unbutton my fatigue shirt with shaking fingers, leaving me clad only in my T-shirt and pants. Working quickly, I rip the shirt in half and wrap one piece over my nose and mouth, tying it in the back of my head to secure the makeshift mask. I scramble to my feet and grab Xandyr’s arm, pulling him to the ground beside me.

He blinks away his tears as I tie the second half of my shirt around the lower part of his face. His hands seem not to be in his control as he bats futilely at me, with no effect. Finally, his hands drop to his lap, and he sits there blinking at me in confusion.

"Mmphhmph!"

I can't tell if he can't speak because of the gas I now realize has been released into the air, or because I've tied his mask too tight. I loosen the knot, giving him a little more air.

At this point, though, more air isn't necessarily a good thing.

"They've gassed us with something," I say loudly, even though to my ears the words are muffled. Mask or gas? "There's something in the air. It's affecting our emotions, and probably our perceptions. We can't trust anything we see."

Xandyr wipes his sleeve across his eyes. He slumps back against the wall as a momentary look of defeat crosses his face.

It doesn't last.

He straightens up, eyes hard, and places a firm hand on my shoulder.

"Thanks, Kai," he says shakily. "If you hadn't realized..."

"No problem," I say. "I've got your back."

"I've heard they were experimenting with hallucinogens on soldiers, but I didn't think it had gone this far. We can't trust anything we see."

"Or anything we feel."

Is paranoia an effect of the gas? I suddenly wonder if they've been dosing us all the way along. Is what I feel for Xandyr real or the product of being drugged?

It doesn't really matter right now. I need to work with him as my commanding officer, and my friend. We can figure out if what we have been feeling is real when we get out of this.

"We need to find the queen," I say, pulling him to his feet. "My mother."

I feel my own eyes start to fill, but this time it's Xandyr who draws me back to reality.

"We will," he says firmly. "Stay close. And remember that as real as this looks, it's all an artificial environment. Nothing is real."

He heads for the tunnel opening and slips out into the overgrown grass surrounding the castle ruins. I follow on his heels, moving forward while covering our backs with my laser rifle. We race toward the corner of the structure, peek around the broken masonry, then run-walk another hundred yards to an opening in the broken wall.

When we duck inside the walls, the light dims. They're making this environment as difficult as possible while still being entertaining. A buzzing above our heads captures my attention and I swing my rifle upwards.

"No," Xandyr places his hand on the barrel of my rifle, forcing it down. "Don't waste your shot."

Looking closer, I see that the buzzing is coming from a video drone, hovering just above our heads. Capturing every move we make and broadcasting it back to the viewers in Mag City. The voyeurs are eager to watch us die. To watch us kill.

They don't care whose blood is shed as long as they get their show. Of course, the rating will be higher for my death, and for Xandyr's. Enemies of the state.

And for my mother, Queen Helena, the ratings will be the highest of all.

We move carefully into the confines of the ruined castle. I can see by the disturbed foliage of weeds growing up inside that someone has passed this way.

Queen Helena, I think.

I hope.

We follow the beaten down weeds past crumbled walls head-high, past depressions in the ground, past piles of rock. At one point, a gaping hole opens up in the path, and we follow the trail of human footsteps around the black pit yawning in front of us. Probably a cellar. Or at least, that's what it would have been, if this ruin was real and not an AI simulation.

I fall behind when I hear a rustling off to my left, taking a few steps in that direction.

Is my mother hiding in the underbrush?

Using my rifle to push aside the weeds, I peer under the shrubs which have taken root inside the castle walls. Nothing. There's no way to find anyone in here.

"Kai," Xandyr calls out, "we need to stick close together."

He's backtracked to find me so we don't lose each other in the maze of broken stone and overgrown foliage. I nod in agreement, and we move forward again, back-to-back, weapons up and at the ready. As we move into the maze, I can feel a rumbling through the soles of my boots. This must be some weird amalgam of real and virtual environments. Xandyr signals right with a wave of one of his pistols. I follow him into a short corridor of broken walls, then right, into a longer corridor.

After several minutes, Xandyr calls a halt. "We need to figure out how to survive this," he says. "With the bounty on her head, everyone will be gunning for the queen. I know she's your birth mother, but if you allow sentimentality to determine your actions, we'll all end up dead. And I intend to survive this thing, both of us."

"She's my mother!" I shout, my emotions rising to overwhelm me again. "I'm not going to let her be killed because she saved my life!"

Xandyr shoves his pistol into the waistband of his pants as he turns back to me. He reaches for my face, and I bat his hands away. He's one of the monsters who lured me here, lured me to Mag City so that I could be killed for their entertainment. I turn to run but he tackles me, pinning me to the ground. Feel his hands at my face. He's trying to choke me.

"Kai! Kai!" He shout-whispers, hands on my shoulders as he crushes me into the dirt with the weight of his body. "Your mask! Pull up your mask!"

Somehow his words make an impression on my muddled mind. I reach up and discover that the torn shirt has slipped down, leaving my nose bare. I pull it up again, and Xandyr tightens the knot on the back of my head.

I've been breathing the drugged air for I don't know how long.

It's barely minutes before my mind starts to clear again.

"I'm...I'm sorry," I say at last. "I'm just worried about the queen. We have to find her. She's my mother. She did what she did to save the life of one of her children." I'm still fighting off the effects of the hallucinogenic gas. "I can't abandon her."

He shakes his head. "No one will care about that," he says. "All they see is that she never objected to this whole corrupt system. She is equally guilty for allowing this to continue, for dividing us by the colors of our blood."

"I don't care," I say. "She risked her life to save mine,"

"You'll die to save her then!"

He doesn't understand.

He can't understand.

I stare at him for another long moment before I shake my head and push him away. We don't have time to argue now. I scramble to my feet again, checking to make sure my mask is secure. We can't afford to lose any more time on emotional outbursts and paranoid delusions.

All our lives are in danger.

I take off in the direction I'm sure Queen Helena went, feet pounding the ground as I run crouching down a long corridor, swinging my rifle from side to side.

Halfway along, I see a shadow disappear into an opening and race in that direction.

The opening leads into a small room, its domed roof still intact. A muddy figure crouches against the far wall, cowering in abject terror. I've found my mother.

"Queen Helena!"

She whips around pointing the blast gun at my chest, her finger on the trigger. Xandyr jumps between us and kicks the barrel of the queen's gun upwards. Her shot hits the ceiling far overhead, sending a rain of dust down on our heads. Shakily, she focuses on my face and doesn't fire a second time.

Xandyr pulls off his own shirt and tears it in half, wrapping one piece around my mother's face for a mask and shoving the other half into his waistband. No doubt there will be someone else who needs it as we move through this maze of hallucinogen-assisted computer simulations.

I can see from the look in her eyes that the queen's mind is clearing quickly now that she's not breathing the gas.

"Kairyn! Oh, my god! I nearly—"

"It's ok," I say, equally shakily. "Good reflexes, Your Majesty."

She swings the gun onto her shoulder by the strap, nestling it in the curve of her underarm. “Kairyn—and you, too Sergeant—you should call me Helena. I won’t ask you to call me Mom,” Helena turns back to me, “since you have a mother, back in Eie. But I’m no longer the queen, as I understand it. My husband has put a price on my head. I believe that means I’m no longer a member of the royal family.”

I swallow hard, touched by this. “Okay, then, Helena. Thank you.”

My birth father might want me dead, but Helena is another story.

“We need to stick together,” Xandyr says. Thankfully, he’s coming around to my need to protect my mother. “Your Maj—*Helena*. We’ll get through this if we watch each other’s backs.”

“I’m not totally incompetent,” she says, laughing ruefully. “I didn’t do too badly in my own Transcendent Hunt, even if it was eighteen years ago. I scored high enough to catch Prince Ilan’s eye, after all. Although, now that I think about it, maybe that wasn’t the best outcome.”

I step closer to her, helping her up from the ground. She leans back against the wall, her legs shaking, but her eyes are definitely clearing. She lifts her free hand to push the fall of hair back from my forehead. Her eyes seem filled with mist.

What a place for a mother and child reunion.

"I don't regret my marriage, though. Never think that! It gave me Hern and you, even if I couldn't keep you."

Xandyr steps forward then. "I hate to break this up, ladies," he says, "but we need to figure out how to survive this."

At least he's come over to my side. He'll help me protect the queen.

Just then, the ruined walls start to move around us. The wall Helena is leaning against melts away while the opening we came through slides shut behind us. For a moment, none of us moves.

"What if it's rigged," I ask Xandyr, "to lead in the direction they want us to go?"

Xandyr laughs harshly. "I have no doubt that's exactly what's going on."

"And they'll lead us into danger," Helena says. "The king wants me dead. I betrayed him. My very existence is an embarrassment to him."

"You and me both!" I think about the terms he set for this Second Hunt. "Everyone will be gunning for us. They won't even consider working together so that we all survive."

“Is that what you were thinking in the Transcendent Hunt?” Helena asks. “That was brilliant! Stupid, but brilliant.”

“How am I supposed to kill my friends now?” I turn to Xandyr. “How do we survive against the best-trained troop the Hunt has ever seen? If they even have any feelings for us, if they want to help us, the gas will screw with their minds until they can’t tell what’s real and what’s an illusion.”

“I’ve been thinking about that,” he says, his eyes focused on the new corridor in case someone approaches. “We are both excellent shots. We shoot to wound, not to kill. The wounded will be removed from the arena, or at least they won’t still be able to pursue us.” He turns to my mother. “You just do your best, I know it’s been a while since your training. We won’t hold it against you if you need to shoot to kill.”

Our plan laid, we take up a triangular formation, with me and Xandyr in front and my birth mother behind us. We move quickly down the corridor that appeared out of the ruined castle, turning right or left when the walls shift. We reach a straight corridor, enclosed on all sides. The setting shifts, the tumbled stones of the castle ruin blending into the featureless gray walls of another tunnel.

We still haven’t seen another person since we separated at the beginning of this Hunt. But they have to be here.

Somewhere.

Searching for us. Searching for me.

Ready to kill me.

Chapter Twenty-four

OUR GUARD NEVER WAVERS as we approach the end of the tunnel and scope out the next challenge in our path.

It's another natural environment. Unlike the overgrown foliage surrounding the castle ruins though, this one is far more threatening.

With the knowledge that even AI simulations can be deadly, we step out into the environment and immediately sink up to the tops of our boots in murky, muddy water.

Xandyr and I exchange a meaningful look. It's a swamp we're standing in, overgrown and fetid. The stench of decaying things rises up around us with every step. I reach out with my free hand to stop Xandyr's forward progress.

"Wait," I say. "What are we...what can happen here? How real is this?"

Xandyr looks worried, although he's trying to stay cool.

“As real as we believe?” he says. “Remember, we have already been exposed to whatever that gas was. I have no doubt we are affected in some way, our perceptions altered. At least we have the ability to understand that what we’re seeing or experiencing is probably not real. That might help us.”

But as we move out into the swamp in search of the next tunnel, I swear the warm water sloshing over the tops of my boots and soaking my socks is real. I look back at Helena. She is pale. Shaken.

She doesn’t like this at all.

None of us do.

But for a woman who has lived her life in the safety and security of the palace, in the very lap of luxury, this must be sheer hell.

I turn forward again, following in Xandyr’s footsteps. We’re moving single file now. I drop back to take the rear, putting Helena in between us.

We try to aim for the opposite side of the simulation. It should be a straight path, but we keep having to veer around moss-draped tree trunks, pools of fetid water, and obvious patches of quicksand.

Xandyr is right. We need to treat this as if it is real, all of it.

The sweat rolling down my face is certainly real. My sleeve is soaked where I use it to wipe my forehead, to stop the salty sweat from stinging my eyes.

There are even the sounds of insects buzzing and birds flash through the trees overhead, flitting from branch to branch. But I only realize those creatures are there when the constant noise of their foraging dies away into silence.

Xandyr holds up a hand, stopping our forward movement. We drop into a crouch, all of us still in a row. Helena looks back at me with fear in her eyes.

She's the weak link.

But I will protect her. I owe her.

Suddenly, Xandyr signals left. We need to get off the path. All together, we scurry low into the underbrush, taking cover. Just in time.

Four of our Purple teammates—Wadyn, Radyn, Dell, and Heryd—approach our hiding place from behind. If the birdsong hadn't died away to warn us, we would have been caught out in the open. Queen Helena lifts her blast gun in front of her face, tracking the Purples' movements. It's awkward for me to maneuver my laser rifle in the tight space, so I shift my weight back, allowing me room to raise my longer gun.

That shift backwards saves me. The extra space keeps me from being hit by a blast of plasma fire when an unseen teammate opens fire on the twins and their other two companions in a wide burst of laser fire.

Xandyr somehow senses it coming, his senses honed by years of training. He dives to cover Helena, knocking her flat and covering her with his body. Wadyn, Radyn, Dell, and Heryd take cover behind tree trunks, returning fire. I follow the direction their weapons are pointing through the steamy air and catch a glimpse of a Blue badge.

It's now or never. I have an open line of fire from behind and to the left of the Purples' positions. My hands are shaking slightly as I sight down the barrel of my rifle.

Shoot to wound, not to kill.

I aim for their feet.

Pull the trigger.

And tear up the mud their feet are fast sinking into.

The Purples' screams of pain tear up my soul. They scramble for cover, but I see trails of blood running down their legs, out of the sides of their boots. I didn't miss.

All four of the Purples are wounded, not fatally. But they're out of the competition.

While they're scrambling for cover, Xandyr waves us on. Helena follows him in the direction of that Blue badge I saw a few seconds ago. Without warning, Dantil, the Blue boy from Ara, drops from the trees to land behind me. I swing my rifle up to sight on him, but he kicks it away. My weapon goes flying into the underbrush.

Dantil barrels into me, knocking me flat on my back. I grab for the long hunting knife he's holding at my throat, but he outweighs me, and I can't get leverage in the slippery mud smeared over his entire body. He pins me with the knife ready to slice my jugular.

"About time you showed up, Kai!" He laughs softly, then pulls his knife away. "We've been waiting for you two."

"You three," a girl's voice comes from above my head and I crane my neck backwards to discover Emvy, from Elm, standing beside Queen Helena. She nods at Helena respectfully.

"We'd better get moving," Xandyr turns back to our little group. He's been watching our trail, back to where I wounded the four Purples. "Good to see you two again."

"The rest of the Blues spaced themselves out," Emvy says. "We've been watching each pod for you two to show up.

Teamwork, right?"

The Blues? "What about the Purples?" I ask. "Are they—"

"All gone over to the king's side," Dantil says. "We knew it would be that way. When it comes down to it, they only care about improving their own positions in this corrupt society."

"We decided that whatever happens," Emvy goes on, "us Blues would stick together. Along with the Sarge here, and you, Kai."

As we search for the tunnel out of the swamp pod, we hear sporadic gunfire from elsewhere across the arena complex. Blues wounding Purples to take them out of the competition? Or Purples killing their former teammates to gain power and money?

The thought of all the blood being shed here to satisfy the king's twisted plan for continued domination is sickening.

Finally, we find the tunnel entrance concealed behind some huge ferns and race through it single file. Our next challenge is open marshland, with brackish water up to our shoulders and brown grasses waving overhead. We hold our weapons above the water as we cross.

Not long into the marsh, a loud splash signals some new danger. Are there Purples hiding just ahead? Our forward movement slows as we wait to see what will appear.

“Arrgh!” I can’t hold back my groan of pain. Something beneath the murky water has latched onto my thigh. “Help me! Xandyr! Somebody—!”

Dantil appears at my side. “What is it?”

“My leg—” I gasp. “Biting me—”

“You’re okay, Kai.” Xandyr wraps his free arm around my waist, supporting my weight as I lean on him to lift my right leg, covering the marsh ahead with his weapon. Emvy grabs for my boot as I lift my leg, helping me get my leg above the water.

A cayman—a small crocodile—has latched onto my thigh, its needle-sharp teeth piercing my thigh a hundred times. Dantil grabs the flailing tail, lifting the creature into the air and stabbing it repeatedly in the abdomen until finally it releases its jaws. I’m shaking, in shock, as Dantil flings it away into the tall grass.

I thought all of this was AI, a simulation. But the blood pouring from my thigh is very real.

Helena shoves in beside me, pulling off her shirt, leaving her wearing just a thin T-shirt.

“Lift her up,” she orders. Our other three companions raise me out of the water, their arms beneath my back, butt, and legs. Helena swiftly wraps her shirt around my wounded thigh, stopping the flow of fresh blood into the water.

As real as this simulation is, my blood might attract other predators. We need to get out of here.

Another tunnel. Another environment.

I'm getting weaker as I feel the poison of the fetid water infecting me with gods know what. I limp along through a rock field of sharpened stones, where we see streaks of blood staining the stone surfaces. Black streaks from laser fire score the rocks here and there. There was a major firefight here.

We pick up three more Blues here, hiding among the rocks. Nria, Merisa, and Cylix join our band. It seems like our original ploy is resurrecting itself. We're working together, the Blues, at least.

No wonder. The Blue Blooded have the most to lose.

There are more drones hovering above, filming us. Sending footage of our struggles back to the voyeurs in Mag City.

King Ilan must be throwing a fit.

He tried to break us apart.

He tried to break us down.

But we've proven yet again that we can't be broken.

Chapter Twenty-five

THE NEXT POD WE enter reminds me of home. Green forest land. More birds singing in the trees. Crickets chirping in the underbrush. Frogs croaking in a pond somewhere nearby.

We don't let our guard down for an instant.

My leg is throbbing from the bite. When I untie Helena's shirt and peel back the torn fabric of my pants, the skin is swollen around the bloody teeth marks. For a simulation, this is frighteningly real.

One of the hovering drones zips in, taking up a position directly overhead. I hear a buzzing as the camera lens repositions itself, staring directly into the bloody mess. What are they seeing? Is my leg intact on the feed?

It doesn't seem possible.

The gas they've released into the complex is really screwing with my mind. And, no doubt, with everyone else's. Nria pulls out a water bottle and pours it over my thigh, washing away the blood and mud.

I gasp with pain.

This *has* to be real.

It's Cylix this time who peels off his fatigue shirt and uses it to rewrap my wound. Merisa finds a stick for me to use as a crutch and, after a bit of work with the knife she found at the beginning of this hunt, she cleans off the small branches.

Xandyr and Helena help me to my feet, and I balance on the stick; I can barely put my weight on my damaged leg. "You should leave me behind," I tell them. "Get to the end. Save yourselves. You can come back for me."

"No." Xandyr's word is abrupt, but I know he's afraid for me. For all of us. "We stick together. No one is leaving anyone behind. We're stronger in a group."

He organizes everyone, a phalanx of weapons sweeping the area, with Helena and me in the center. I can't carry my rifle while I hobble along on the stick, and it's too heavy for my mother, so I trade it for Xandyr's plasma pistol, tucking the smaller weapon in my waistband. We set off into the dimming forest as fast as possible.

I try not to hold everyone back, but I am moving much slower now, my head throbbing as much as my leg. Beside me on the path, Helena is shaking her head as if she has a bug in her ear. The light above us is growing dimmer.

Is it late afternoon already?

I look up when something falls on my cheek, brushing the feather-light touch away. Wet. *Cold.* Suddenly, we're in the midst of a heavy snowfall, the ground whitening beneath our boots.

The ground begins to rise, trees falling away as the path grows rocky. Huge boulders loom on all sides and we slow further as we fight our way through the maze, boots slipping on the now-icy surface.

We're forced to go single file. Without warning, I see the boy in front of me—Cylix—fall to the ground. Blue blood stains the back of his T-shirt.

Shot.

I drop beside him as everyone scatters, seeking cover in the snow-covered rocks. Cylix's eyes are wide open. Staring.

Dead.

If I had been two feet further up the path it would have been me.

I gasp back a sob. Another death. Another life lost because of me.

My mind flashes back to River. He died because he followed me here. Now others are dying because of my clever planning in the Transcendent Hunt.

It won't end until I'm dead myself.

I push myself to my feet, bracing my weight on the stick, and stand swaying among the rocks.

"Here!" I scream into the swirling whiteness of the artificial blizzard. "I'm here! Just kill me now and let the others go!"

Am I screaming at the other Sixteens? At the Purples I shared quarters and training with? Or am I screaming at my father, the king of Elleon, who wants me erased from his world?

I see the red dot of a laser sight appear through the air, tracking a trail through the snow to center on my chest. I lift my arms wide to either side. Angel wings. In my next life, that's all I can hope for.

I'm thrown backwards by the blast, hitting my head on a rock.

Everything goes black.

“Am I dead?”

A bitter laugh resounds through the darkness.

“Not yet,” Xandyr says. I hear him moving, but I can’t see anything until he lifts my head and unwraps a piece of fabric from around my head. “You might wish you were, though,” he goes on, “when you try to sit up. I think you might have a concussion.”

“Concuss...?”

“Yeah, sorry about that,” he says, lifting a bottle of water to my lips. I sip gratefully, the water icy cold in my parched throat. “I kind of knocked you into the rocks so you didn’t get seared. Galea was hiding ahead of us, along with Jeaol, Beva, Xion, and Kela. Galea killed Cylix, and she would have killed you.”

The Purple girl was one of the nicest recruits back in the training complex.

I feel tears prickle in the corners of my eyes.

“And the others...?”

“Dead. I’m sorry, Kai,” Xandyr says, not meeting my eyes.

He killed five of his own trainees, to save me. And my birth mother.

I struggle to sit up in Xandyr's arms. He shifts, lifting me to rest my back against his chest, his arms encircling me from behind. He is little protection from the bone-chilling cold. At least now I'm so cold that I can't feel my torn thigh.

I can hardly feel anything.

We are huddled in a sort of rock cave, huge boulders surrounding us, keeping the snow off our heads. Outside a narrow opening, I can see that the snow has piled up, several feet high now. And the wind has picked up, blowing small drifts into our meager shelter.

"Where's Helena? The others?"

I can feel Xandyr shaking his head, but it hurts too much to turn and look him in the face. Reaching up, I can feel an egg-sized lump on the back of my head.

"No idea," Xandyr says. "I barely got you under cover."

I fall silent. It's too difficult to think. Too hard to talk. It feels like my jaw is frozen.

I tuck my hands into my armpits for warmth. Is it possible to get frostbite from a simulation? Probably. The bite wound I got in the marsh environment certainly feels real.

Shuddering, I huddle closer to him. “How can this be so realistic?”

“I don’t know. Whatever gas it is they’ve dosed us with has totally messed with our perceptions.” He falls silent for a few minutes. When he speaks again, the chill in my bones deepens. “If we are experiencing this all to this extent, I have no doubt that what we think is happening could kill us as easily as any laser fire or plasma bullets.”

In the cold, I feel my consciousness slipping away again. Xandyr shakes me.

“Wha—what?”

“Stay awake, Kai,” he says. “If you fall asleep you might not wake up.”

“How long do we have to stay here?”

“I don’t know. You just need to rest. But don’t go to sleep. I’m hoping they give up on us and stop the simulation. Stop dumping snow on us.”

I don’t know if that will ever happen. I’m done. Despite my best efforts, I fall into a deep sleep, and nothing Xandyr does can wake me again.

I don't know how long I slept, but Xandyr was right about the environment.

When I wake, the rocks and snow are gone.

I am lying cradled in his arms on a featureless gray floor. The curved walls of the pod rise above us, where several drones hover noiselessly. At my first movements, they blink into wakefulness, focusing their camera eyes on Xandyr and me.

Sitting up slowly, I look around. On the far side of the pod, I see two guards carrying a body between them, arms hanging down, fingertips brushing the floor.

Cylix.

No one else is in the pod.

As the two guards exit through a door in the wall, I hear the gas start to spit and a cloud fills the air.

Not again.

I pull the hem of my T-shirt up over my nose and shake Xandyr awake.

He's so groggy. He must have been knocked out while I slept.

“Wha...where...?”

“We’re still in the hunt arena,” I say, pulling his mask up over his nose. “We need to find Helena!”

Xandyr pulls himself upright groggily, looking around. He isn’t surprised at the blank walls. “Come on,” he says, grabbing me by the hand. “We need to get to the end.”

I can’t help but wonder how lucky we are that no one came upon us while we were out cold. But I also have to wonder why we’re still alive.

My leg is still throbbing, but walking seems a bit easier. I can’t take the time to check my wound, though. Not now.

Not when we might finally be reaching the end.

It doesn’t matter if what I perceive is real or hallucinatory.

I just need to power through.

Nothing else matters.

Chapter Twenty-six

THE NEXT POD WE enter is underwater. An ocean seascape, with coral reefs and fish swimming through the air. It feels so real!

We fight for several tense moments to calm our breathing. We *can* breathe. It's not really water we're walking through. We've got this.

The trio of great white sharks that swim at us with gaping jaws and razor sharp teeth, though, we fire at immediately. Who knows what real damage they could do? After my cayman bite, we're not taking any chances.

The blood they trail in the water as they thrash certainly seems real. And we increase our speed to reach the tunnel on the other side as quickly as we can.

We pass through one more pod—a pit of bubbling mud, which we cross on tilting log-lashed rafts—before we enter a long tunnel, three times the length of any of the others. We haven't encountered any more of the Sixteens, friends or enemies—

Blues or Purples—but they must be here somewhere. Granted, they may have circled through the pods in the opposite direction from the way we'd taken. Or the pods may not even be placed in a circle, but more of an interconnected maze.

There's no way to know.

Still, we keep our guard up.

The end of the long tunnel is sealed off by sliding glass doors. In front of the doors, armed guards await us.

"Place your weapons in the bins," a masked guard orders, pointing through the closed door to a barrel placed to one side. Inside it there are numerous weapons—rifles, pistols, crossbows, and staffs—all chucked in on top of each other. We add ours to the cache.

As we turn back to the doors, the glass panels slide open and the guard steps forward.

"Glad to see you made it, Sargeant Krim," she says in a low voice. She discreetly flips back the collar of her uniform to reveal a tiny piece of blue cloth sewn into the facing. Our eyes meet and she nods. "And you, Kairyn."

This guard, at least, seems sympathetic. "The queen...?" I ask in a whisper.

“Safe,” she says, nodding behind her to the center of the main arena. We’ve circled back to where we began. From here, we can see other survivors, huddled in the center of the space. My birth mother is in the center of a cluster of Blues. A few pockets of Purples surround them menacingly, but no one is fighting.

My mother perks up when she spots us near the doors.

I hobble across the width of the floor to Helena, reaching out to hug her. “I was so scared...!”

“Kairyn! Thank goodness you’re all right! When we got separated in the snowstorm—” Helena hugs me back, tightly.

“What happens now?” I ask, but she shakes her head.

“It won’t be good, whatever Ilan has planned.” Helena’s face is strained. She is filthy, like the rest of us, her clothing torn and muddied.

But we made it through alive. We have to be thankful for that.

Our second Hunt has ended.

From what I can see, our numbers are less than half what they were when we started. I know that I wounded several Purples. They were removed from the arena. And Xandyr killed at least five of his own trainees. Cylix, the Blue boy who helped me, was dead.

And who knew how many others?

It seems we're about to find out.

Those huge screens descend from the ceiling again, but this time they're displaying different numbers.

Beside each of our names, there are three scores.

Killed. Wounded.

And the bounties earned.

Sergeant Krim: Three wounded. Five killed. Bounty $297,500.

Kairyn of Eie: Four killed. Bounty $184,700.

Wait! No! That's wrong!

I wounded those four Purples. I fired at their feet. I didn't kill them.

More screens lower to eye level around the main arena, circling the walls. On each is footage of the Hunt inside the pods, highlights of the action.

I see Purples and Blues attacking each other in a myriad of different environments.

Killing.

Wounding.

As we watch the carnage play out, there's one thing I notice.

When it's Blues attacking Purples, they seem to be holding back. Wounding, not killing.

When it's the Purples, though, the tactics are far different. The Purple Sixteens go for the kill. When they just injure an opponent, they take the time to torture their victims, inflicting horrific wounds over and over, mutilating and defacing their bodies.

Is this what we really are, the people of Elleon? Sadistic monsters?

No wonder no one in the ruling class wants to see the Transcendent Hunt brought to an end.

I finally find the screen showing my encounter in the swamp. The footage shows Wadyn, Radyn, Dell, and Heryd, firing at me. And me firing back, shooting the mud at their feet. They dive for cover. Wounded, not killed.

But then the footage changes. A camera focuses on my face, calm and blank, no human expression to be seen. I run forward through the swamp to the Purples' position. They lie cowering behind tree trunks, begging for their lives.

The footage—obviously doctored—shows me using a spear to run them through, pinning each one to the ground, impaled on the point. Radyn tries to crawl away, and I plant the spear in her spine, leaving her flailing helplessly, her face in the swamp water, until I pull out a knife and slit her throat from ear to ear. Her blood flows out into the water around her in gentle eddies as she sinks into the mud.

Her twin, Wadyn, crawls to her, crying out his sister's name. I plant my boot on his chest, holding him back while he begs for his life. Then I plunge my knife into his abdomen over and over until his ropy intestines spill out on the ground.

But I didn't have a knife.

I didn't have a spear.

I didn't kill Wadyn and Radyn, or Dell and Heryd.

It's all fake footage.

Xandyr comes up behind me as I stand there in shock, my mouth hanging open. He wraps an arm around my shoulders, turning me away from the carnage playing out over and over in a constant loop.

“That wasn’t you,” he says. “That wasn’t you.”

“Did I? I’d remember...” tears begin to stream down my face. “That wasn’t me!”

“No, Kai, it wasn’t you,” he agrees. “And if that wasn’t you,” he goes on, “then it probably wasn’t any of them.”

He waves a hand to indicate the other screens.

Maybe none of it happened.

But maybe it did.

We were all gassed with a hallucinatory agent that skewed our perceptions. Who can say what we did—or didn’t do—under its effects?

Without warning, the hologram of the king and Prince Hern appears again in the center of the arena.

“Congratulations to the high scorers in the first half of this Second Hunt!”

First half?

It’s supposed to be over.

Looking around at the looks on my fellow Sixteens' faces, I see dawning horror. None of us are meant to survive this. We let ourselves be lulled by reaching this point, thinking the ordeal was over, the bounties awarded.

But it's not over yet.

The screens rise back to the ceiling, and one wall flips completely around, revealing a row of doors. These doors slide open to reveal small chambers with identical white uniforms hanging from pegs on the walls.

"There are twenty of you left," King Ilan continues. Behind him, Prince Hern looks gray. Sickened. "Now you will go one on one in the second half of this competition. Each of you will receive identical weaponry: a laser blaster with enough juice for one hundred shots. You will be indistinguishable in your new uniforms, so there is no chance of complicity. Kill or be killed. That is your choice."

I look around at the frightened faces of the other Sixteens, Purple and Blue alike. At Xandyr. At Helena.

The king has arranged this so that no one can work together.

I will fire to defend myself, but what if I shoot my birth mother?

Or the man I am falling in love with?

I won’t do it!

“Guards!” The king calls out from his holographic podium. “Herd the contestants into their chambers to change. If any resist, shoot them.”

A row of guards has appeared behind us while we stood transfixed. Now they hold their plasma rifles in front of them as they move towards us, herding us each through a door.

“Xandyr!” I yell as I try to hold onto his arm and pull him inside with me. One of the guards moves in and brings the butt of his rifle down on our shoulders, battering until we let go of each other. I am thrown through one of the doors and fall hard onto the cement floor, bruising my injured shoulder further. I lie there for a moment, but there may only be minutes to spare before we are forced into this fresh hell.

I pull myself upright. Peel off my filthy, sweat-soaked clothes.

My thigh is still bleeding, the bite marks almost indistinguishable in the swollen, infected flesh.

It was a real bite. From a real monster.

It had to be.

I shrug into the new uniform, pulling the legs of the bottom half of the one-piece suit on carefully. Pull the arms on and zip it from crotch to neck. There's an attached hood which covers my head completely, with a piece of black mesh fabric covering my face, along with white gloves and white boots.

Once I'm dressed, there's nothing to distinguish me from anyone else, except maybe my height and weight.

Will Xandyr know who I am? How could he?

I won't know who he is, in the arena.

I could shoot him and never know what I'm doing.

I could shoot my mother.

It's just moments after I attach the gloves to the ends of my sleeves and pick up my weapon that a door on the opposite side from the first one slides open. I step out slowly, crouched low to present a smaller target.

I enter a narrow corridor, formed of shoulder-high white blocks. After ten feet or so, the corridor ends and I stop, crouching against the wall while I survey this new environment. The setting I am entering is like something out of one of the video games we've trained on.

There are a series of walls of differing heights and lengths. As I watch, I see heads ducking behind the barriers, arms and legs flashing as combatants dodge from one hiding place to the next.

At the far side of the enormous space, a row of blinking lights signals the end of this section of the course.

I have to reach that side alive.

It's only moments before the firing starts.

Ribbons of amber laser fire erupt from the rifles, each bullet trailing a stream of light. I only have a hundred shots. I need to conserve ammo. I move out carefully into the labyrinth, every sense on high alert.

I've only gone thirty yards or so when someone darts at me from the left. He doesn't see me—I say "he" because of the height, although there are a couple of very tall girls among us—because his blaster is slow to rise. I don't recognize Xandyr's stance as the white-clad combatant. So, I swing my weapon up and pull the trigger.

Nothing.

No fire.

I bang the blaster with the palm of my hand, trying to correct the glitch, but when I pull the trigger again, nothing happens.

My opponent seizes the few seconds I've wasted trying to fire at him to aim at my head.

I kick out with a white-booted foot and connect with his weapon, sending it flying off over the barricades. My next kick snaps his right forearm, and he falls to the ground, screaming with pain.

I dart away, taking cover behind another low wall.

Raising my blaster, I punch the reload button. No lights. No juice.

My blaster is a dud.

In a split second, I know what has happened.

The laser blasters are programmed by computer. They watched me in the changing cubicles and deprogrammed my weapon. I am meant to die here, with no chance of defending myself.

And I'll bet that Helena and Xandyr's weapons are similarly disabled. At least that will provide a clue to who they are in the otherwise indistinguishable uniforms.

In the row of changing cubicles, the one I ended up in was about seventh from the right-side end. I started out closer to the right wall of the arena. Everyone else will likely be drawn to the center of the arena, making as direct a route for the exit in the center of the far wall as possible. It's human nature to take the most direct path.

So, I take a lateral route, cutting right. I'll hit the right-hand wall, then head for the far side, cutting left to follow that wall to the door. I'll avoid the crowd heading for the center route. There's no other option. Without a working blaster, I'm a sitting duck.

I can only hope that my mother and Xandyr have the same thought.

My plan works. While I catch occasional glimpses of other combatants popping up around the variety of barricades, I encounter only one other person on my path when a very short, slight female darts into the space directly in front of me.

From the size of her, I know it's Piperell, a Blue from Elm. She was the tiniest of the Sixteen trainees.

"Pip!" I call out when she swings her blaster up, pointing it square in the center of my chest. "It's me! Kai!"

For just a moment, I wonder if I've made a mistake.

I see Piperell's finger tighten on the trigger. My stomach clenches, my shoulders hunching in protectively. Providing a smaller target. But then she turns away, running in a crouch for the next stanchion.

My way is clear. Keeping tight to the wall, I scurry low to the right until I reach the door and duck through.

I am in a long corridor, lined with screens. Panting for breath, I lean a shoulder against one wall, taking a pause to allow my heartrate to return to a calmer level. Then I push on.

Videos play around me, over the long walls and ceiling. It's a cacophony of flashing lights and sounds, impossible to decipher. I cringe, under attack by the images.

Interspersed with the footage of the games—of my doctored attack on the Purples—is footage from villages around Elleon. I see Oma's shocked face, mouth gaping, as she watches me killing Wadyn, Radyn, and the others. She is obviously sickened by what she's seeing. Those seated near her in the village barn turn away, shunning her. There is no sympathy for the mother of a killer.

She vomits on the floor, then stumbles outside, disappearing into the brilliant sunshine.

My poor mother.

What I see is bad enough, playing out over and over. But the thought of what Oma must be going through, seeing me with Queen Helena—my birth mother—rips my heart out.

I don't know who I am anymore. Oma is horrified to be the mother who raised me. I can never go back to Eie.

Queen Helena is probably dead somewhere behind me, along with Xandyr. My Xandyr.

If I ever get out of here, if I somehow survive this, there will be no place for me in Elleon. The best I can hope for is to escape to an uninhabited place out in the wilderness, to live off the land, scrabbling for survival.

Maybe the Red Bloods will take me in. Maybe they'll let me fight for their cause. I certainly have the training to help them, after being through these abominable Hunts.

I stumble down the corridor, surrounded by pain and terror.

With no warning, a familiar face looms around me, filling all of the screens, repeated in a stream to the end of the corridor.

It's River.

Turning away, I try to escape the image. But he's there… everywhere.

River.

River.

River.

River.

River.

Inside that shadowy abandoned building in Springfield.

Facing the camera.

River's grim face softens when he sees someone enter the building. The camera swings around, the drone following the action. Onscreen, I see my face. On a split-screen view, River smiles, relieved to see me.

But that's not how it happened.

I'm beginning to wonder if I really know the truth of any of this.

Reaching out to touch River's ten-foot-tall face with trembling fingertips, I choke back a sob. "River..." the whisper escapes despite my efforts to contain it.

I suddenly realize that I am being watched, even now. Recorded. Broadcast throughout Elleon. The anonymity of my white uniform is no protection. Everyone knows who I am. Everyone wants to see me suffer.

Stepping back, I watch as the footage of me and River in Springfield, in the Transcendent Hunt, continues to play out. In my hand is the glittering blade of a laser dagger. Even as River gazes into my eyes with relief—with *love*—I plunge the blade of white-hot light into his stomach.

My *image* plunges the blade of white-hot light into his stomach.

Slices upwards as his ropy guts spill out onto a filthy floor covered in broken glass. Watch as his eyes widen in shock. In terror. Stands over River's body as he crumples to the ground, clutching his intestines, trying to contain them.

But it wasn't me.

It wasn't me!

It *isn't* me!

None of this is real. I know it didn't happen this way. It was a Purple Hunter who killed my friend.

It isn't real.

But...

How can I know what's real now? They've twisted everything we believe in, twisted our minds, our perceptions. There's no way I can fight them.

Dropping to my knees, I wrap my arms around my head.

“I give up!” I scream for the cameras. “I give up! You win!”

I feel a boot prod my side. “Get up,” a harsh voice orders.

Raising my head, I find a trio of guards surrounding me. They must have entered the corridor when I was screaming. I never heard them coming. Two of the guards grab me by my arms and force me to my feet, holding me between them.

“Shut it down!” one of them shouts out, and the screens ranging the length of the corridor go black. “Move,” he orders, and they begin dragging me along the floor to the door at the far end.

I can barely keep my feet under me, stumbling along between them.

The guards shove me through the door, and I find myself outdoors under the cloud-filled sky. The weather has turned threatening while we were fighting for our lives in the Second Hunt.

It’s almost poetic.

We’re behind the arena building, in a large field divided into small enclosures by ten-foot-high cattle fences. Through the slatted fenced-in areas, I can see other Sixteens in white uniforms. Their masked hoods are thrown back over their shoulders.

I catch glimpses of parts of faces, but can't see anyone clearly.

An eye, wide open and terrified.

A mouth, open and panting.

A red cheek streaked with tears.

The guards wrestle me through a gate into an empty pen as if I'm livestock being led to slaughter. The gate locks firmly shut behind me, the metal ringing. This is how the Second Hunt ends. Was always meant to end. With the survivors penned until we can be executed.

Remember your training, I hear Xandyr's voice in my head. Xandyr.

Is he okay?

Looking outside, I scope out the set up. A framework of catwalks runs along the outside of the animal pens. Armed guards patrol, their plasma weapons held at the ready. At the slightest disturbance they'll unload on us.

The clouds are piling up overhead. A storm is moving in. They can't keep us here for long. If lightning strikes nearby, we'll all be electrocuted, Sixteens and guards alike. The first frozen drops of rain begin spitting down on our heads as the wind picks up.

A part of me is so tired of this. Fighting for my life. Fighting for *all* of our lives. I want to give up.

I want to give in.

They've killed my birth mother in their arena. There's no way she survived against my well-trained companions.

Xandyr must be dead, as well.

I am alone.

No, I chastise myself. I can't think like that. Xandyr and Helena will be okay. They have to be.

Despite all that I've lost, I can't give up.

Sudden shouts ring out from the far side of the fenced-in area, and I take the risk of climbing up the slats of my cattle pen to peer over the top in that direction.

Beneath the gathering cumulonimbus clouds, a wall cloud has formed. Within seconds, a funnel-shaped twister drops down from the wall cloud. A tornado is heading our way.

The guards begin shouting atop their catwalk. The twister is barely miles away and heading straight for us.

Fast.

With no thought for their prisoners, the guards begin running for the ladders, their booted feet pounding the metal walkway. They jump or fall from the catwalk, not even taking the time to climb down. I rise higher on the slatted metal wall of my cage, watching them run for cover. They head for the door into the rear of the arena, leaving us behind.

Leaving us in the path of the tornado.

That would solve King Ilan's problem handily. Let the tornado wipe us from the face of Elleon.

With the soldiers gone, along with their weapons, I keep climbing, up and over the top of the ten-foot-high enclosure. I race along the length of the fenced enclosure, banging my fist against the ringing metal.

"Xandyr. Helena! Everyone, get out!" I scream at the top of my voice, but I'm afraid that the survivors won't hear me over the rising wind. "Tornado coming! Get out!"

Someone has heard me. I see a girl's head pop up over the top of the fence above me.

"Get out! The guards are gone! Climb!"

The toes of booted feet appear between the slats, climbing upwards. My fellow escapees begin to drop from the outside of the fence to the ground. They cluster around me, and we race along the fence. Out of the twenty of us who ended up in the final area of the arena—where we got our white uniforms—I only count seven.

Blues *and* Purples.

Being Purple Blooded doesn't seem to have saved anyone.

King Ilan wants us all dead.

A final head struggles to top the enclosures as we near the end closest to the arena wall.

Helena. She *is* alive!

Picking up speed, I skid to a stop below her as she swings a stiff leg over the top of the metal fence and begins to descend. Without warning a tremendous bolt of lightning crashes into the earth less than a half a mile away, shaking the ground. The downpour starts, needles of rain pounding down on all of us.

I see my mother's hand scrabble for a grip, slide, lose hold—

And she falls backward off the fence.

Rushing forward, we manage to cushion her fall in our midst.

She struggles upward, looking around at us frantically. When she spots me, she bursts into tears.

“Kairyn! Kairyn, my baby! I thought you were—”

I hug her quickly, but there’s no time for catching up. “Have you seen Xandyr? We’ve got to get under cover,” I shout, frantically searching through the curtain of slashing gray for a safe place to hide from the approaching tornado.

“Wait!” I can barely hear Helena over the roar of the oncoming twister. “Sergeant Krim—”

I swing around.

Is Xandyr dead?

He’s not here, but I can’t resign myself to never seeing him again.

But then...

Helena is alive, so—

I finally see that she’s pointing to the enclosure next to one she just climbed out of.

"He was beside me," she puts her mouth next to my ear, yelling loudly. "He's hurt! He can't climb out!"

Running back, I wrestle with the lock on his gate. I can't free him. I don't have the key. There's nothing—

Suddenly one of the others is there. I don't recognize him in the dark rain, his hair plastered to his face. But he's carrying a long piece of metal bar he's found somewhere, which he rams in between the lock and the latch, twisting with inhuman strength to shear off the lock and pop the gate.

I rush inside, followed by my birth mother.

"Xandyr! I'm so sorry!" I cry out at the sight. "Xandyr, what happened to you?"

Xandyr is lying curled on his side, protecting his damaged body from the pouring rain, barely conscious.

"It was the guards," my birth mother says. "They hauled him in here, already broken, then beat him with their truncheons for good measure. All because he went against his orders and tried to save you kids."

I hate this so much. If it weren't for me, and where I came from, he wouldn't be in this position. This is all my fault.

But there's no time to check his condition.

"Help me!" I scream into the storm.

And then the others are there. They could have run for cover, *should* have run for cover. But Sergeant Krim's training—*work together so that we all survive*—is too deeply instilled in them.

Two of the boys, Jae and Del, lift Xandyr's body between them and stumble toward the gate. Outside the enclosure.

And we all run into the storm.

Chapter Twenty-seven

THE DOOR THE FLEEING guards took into the arena is locked. It won't open, despite our frantic pounding.

"This way!" I scream above the growing roar of the approaching twister, waving to the left. The others follow me around the corner of the building. A couple of hundred feet further on, there's a small portico attached to the huge building. I duck inside. There's a staircase leading down into the ground beneath ground level with another wide door at its end. It must be for deliveries or something.

Thank god!

When I try it, the door swings open. "In! In! In!" I scream.

The boys carrying Xandyr go first into the dimly lit basement area. The others follow quickly. When I close the door and turn around, they're all sitting on the floor panting or leaning up against the gray cement wall.

Once again, we've escaped with our lives. But it's not over by a long shot.

The boys lay Xandyr's body on the floor, and I kneel down beside him, turning his face to the dim light from the emergency bulbs overhead. He's bruised and has a streak of dried blood running from his forehead back into his hairline. As I smooth back his rain-wet hair, his eyes open.

He's having trouble focusing, but finally he finds my face, looking into my eyes.

"Kai—"

"I'm here," I say softly. "I'm so sorry. This is all my fault. Are you —"

I pat his torso, looking for major injuries. But he bats my hands away and struggles to pull himself upright.

"I'm fine," he says, but ends with a convulsive cough, cradling his ribcage.

"Probably a broken rib or two, at least."

"How did—?"

"The guards," he says. "I refused to play their game. That last part..." The coughing overtakes him again and it's several seconds before he can speak again. “I went in looking for you, but I couldn’t find you. Everyone else was either dead or through the exit doors when they came for me. I was checking the corpses, afraid...”

“Stupid!” I whisper, and I pull his head into my shoulder, bracing him upright. “You should have gone on. Saved yourself. I’m not worth your life.”

His crooked grin goes straight to my heart.

“There’s nothing worth more in this damned world than you, Kai. I love you.”

Those last words break me, and the tears begin to fall.

It’s hard to believe, but my hard-assed Sergeant has picked this moment in time—just seconds away from annihilation by the tornado bearing down on us—to turn into a romantic fool.

“I love you so much, Xandyr.”

But now it’s too late for us.

Whether it’s King Ilan or the tornado, we are supposed to die.

Not if I can help it.

I stand up then, leaving Xandyr leaning against the wall. Looking around, I try to assess the situation the way he taught us. "We're too close to the door," I say, motioning everyone up. "We need to get further undercover. Quickly!"

"Over here!" Helena has been poking around in the basement through the clutter of machinery. "There's a small mechanical room," she goes on. "It'll provide an extra layer of protection."

I make my way back to Xandyr's side, hooking an arm around his back and pulling his arm over my shoulder. "Someone help me," I call out and one of the other girls, Vala, takes his other side.

It's a struggle to get him up without hurting him further, but we manage. Stumbling along with him between us, we head for where my mother is standing, signaling the direction of the hiding place she's found.

Just in time.

The roaring above us has grown. The shriek of tearing metal resounds above our heads as we duck into the smaller room and Helena slams the door behind us. A huge whoosh of pressure knocks us all to the floor. I land atop Xandyr, trying to protect his head as the emergency lights wink out, leaving us in total darkness.

After all of King Ilan's efforts to destroy us, to eliminate me, it's nature that is going to solve his problem.

This is how my life ends.

It may be minutes, or it may be hours, before I come to after blacking out on top of Xandyr. The walls of the mechanical room around us are intact, but the ceiling is gone.

Along with everything above it.

As I struggle to sit up, aching in every muscle, I do a quick count.

All ten of us survivors...*survived.*

My mother, Queen Helena. Xandyr. Me.

And the seven remaining recruits.

"We need to get out of here," Xandyr says shakily, pulling himself to a sitting position. I take his arm to help him shift upright. "They'll come looking for us. The guards."

But then he glances overhead to the clear blue sky.

The arena is gone, it seems.

He looks back at me. “Someone will come,” he says. “They won’t risk letting any of us go free.”

I nod. “But you...?”

“I can move,” he says. “I think. I have to; we don’t have a choice.”

We assess our conditions and resources quickly, as Sarge taught us.

Resources: none.

Except for our own minds.

Condition: mostly intact. Cuts and bruises. Xandyr’s (possibly) broken ribs. But we can all walk.

It takes a few good shoves to wedge open the door against the debris outside the mechanical room. Looking around, it’s plain to see that the arena took a direct hit from the tornado. The entire thing has been wiped away.

Surveying the damage, though, something doesn’t add up.

The broken floor we’re standing on is at ground level. The outer walls are gone, so I can see directly through the piles of debris to the parking lot that surrounded the arena. Acrid smoke wafts through the open air, choking me. This doesn’t look like the splintered remains of a tornado-ravaged landscape.

It looks like a bomb went off.

Small fires still burn here and there. And the ground is dry, not rain-lashed.

I lead the way through the piles of rubble, supporting Xandyr with his arm over my shoulder. But I stop short when I see a bloody arm in a guard's uniform lying beneath the remains of a wall.

Looking further, I see other body parts, smears of Purple blood darkening the ground.

"This...This wasn't..." I can't force my twisting thoughts into proper sentences.

"It wasn't a tornado," Helena comes up beside me, speaking low. "It was another simulation."

"But the arena—"

The ruined building is real.

Or is it?

The super-high-tech torture chamber, where we fought for our lives, is gone.

We make our way in single file across the floor, now littered with broken pipes and pieces of roof dropped from above. When we finally reach the outside limits of the building, we stop short.

Small piles of debris are littered around the area, but the bulk of the arena is gone. Only one portion of an inner wall remains, and the podium where the holograms of King Ilan and Prince Hern addressed us. Black glass from broken screens litters the ground like shards of ice. Here and there, twisted pipes appear as weird sculptures, something created by a madman.

There is no movement anywhere.

Around the perimeter of the former arena space, however, I see what look like piles of rags scattered around.

More guards. All dead.

“Hey,” one of the others calls out. “Look!”

I whip around and follow her pointing finger. At the far side of what had been a parking lot, among the vehicles tossed about like children’s toys, stands one of the guard busses, intact.

Untouched.

“Let’s go,” Queen Helena orders, taking the lead.

“Where?” I ask her. “Where can we go?” We’re supposed to be dead. We can’t suddenly turn up at home. In Eie. Or Mag City. Or wherever each of us comes from.

“It was a bomb,” Xandyr says, looking back. “I can smell it.”

And I realize that the acrid scent burning my nose and throat is the smell of chemical explosives. While we were fighting for our lives in the arena, rebels have sabotaged the entire complex.

And if they bombed the arena, then—

“We need to go back,” I say. “To Mag City.”

The rebels wouldn’t just attack a remote military training facility. It doesn’t make any sense. This could only have been a distraction.

We all know what their real target would have been.

We need to get back to the city. There’s no way to know what other targets they may have hit while we were fighting for our lives.

Except if we go there.

I look at my mother’s face. She’s terrified. My brother, Prince Hern, was there. In Mag City. In the palace.

But the others...

They come from all over Elleon, from the tiny communities scattered around. Can they go home again? Will they find safe refuge there? Or will they be hunted down and slaughtered?

"I think we need to assess the situation," I say. "That means Mag City." At the round of protests, I raise a hand to signal for silence. "Look, we can't know if we'll ever be safe, if we don't know what the situation with the government is. We need to head for the city first."

"Know your enemy," Xandyr says weakly.

But now...

Is the government of Elleon, King Ilan, our enemy?

Or is it the Red Blood rebels?

Xandyr leans heavily against my side, unable to support himself. I look into his face as he grins weakly. "We need to scope out the lay of the land, and then plan."

I nod in agreement, then lift his arm to my shoulders, wrapping my arm around his waist.

"Somebody help me with him," I say, taking the lead. "Let's see if that bus still works."

Chapter Twenty-eight

ONE OF THE BLUE boys—Jae, from Elm—knows how to drive big vehicles from working with farm equipment, so he manages to get the bus started. It's practically untouched by the bombing, just a few cracked windows.

"Everybody in!" he calls out the door, and we scramble to take our seats. I help Xandyr aboard, then turn and look back one last time at what's left of the arena.

Thank the gods it was destroyed. No one should have to endure what we did in that house of horrors. But I don't know how we ever managed to survive the bombing. The gods are definitely watching our backs.

Jae drives slowly out of the parking area, picking his way around piles of debris. Heading back towards Mag city, the road is clear and we make good time. Until we reach the outskirts of the city.

The destruction there is shocking. It looks like every military or government building has been at least partially damaged by explosives. Some of the largest buildings are nothing but rubble.

There are people outside, milling around, surveying the damage. No one gives our bus a second glance. Luckily, the tinted windows hide us from view. If anyone saw that it was us Sixteens inside—instead of the royal guards—they'd run for their weapons and blast us to flinders.

As we near the palace, the number of people on the streets grows. Soon we can see why.

The palace has taken a direct hit. It must have taken months to plant enough explosives throughout the structure to bring the entire thing down. Roofless walls stand among piles of broken furniture. Intact windows with draperies blowing in the breeze provide a view of...nothingness. Jae pulls the bus through twisted metal gates, unguarded amidst the destruction.

In the gardens in front of the palace, a carved fountain soars into the air, water dancing merrily from one level to the next. Completely untouched by the bombing.

Behind it, the front portico is completely destroyed, nothing more than a pile of white marble shards. We pile out of the bus, looking around in shock.

"We need to find weapons," I say. I spot a broomstick nearby—from the kitchens or housekeeping staff, perhaps—and grab it, handing it to Xandyr to use as a crutch. The others scatter, grabbing whatever they can find to defend ourselves from any guards we come across.

"We need to find my son!" Queen Helena is frantic, heading for the smashed front of the palace.

I grab her arm and pull her back.

"Wait," I say. "We need to be cautious. There's a price on all our heads."

We form up and move slowly through the debris, climbing through a broken floor-to-ceiling window one by one. Inside, the pristine palace is a disaster. The queen leads us to the throne room, but there's no sign of life anywhere.

A door stands open behind a dais where the remains of what were obviously throne-chairs lie smashed into kindling. Scorch marks extend up what remains of the broken walls. The acrid scent of chemical explosives hangs thick in the air.

"Through there," my mother orders. "There's a safe-room. I'm sure that's where Ilan would go, and my son."

I push her behind me and head for the door.

Peering around the edge of the door frame, the remains of a corridor extend roofless toward the rear of the building. The corridor is empty. I enter quickly, followed by the others. The corridor hooks left, and I stop short.

Several guards are lying scattered throughout the hallway. There's no movement.

All dead.

"Hern!" Helena cries out, pushing past me. "These are my son's guards!"

I realize that the dead men and women are dressed in a lighter shade of purple uniforms, not the dark purple of the king's guards. At the end of the hallway a door looms open, darkness beyond. I take cover to one side and push the door further open with my booted foot.

Inside, the room is empty of life.

Among the supply cabinets, cots, and chairs, no one stirs.

This was obviously the king's safe room. But he is gone, along with his guards. And his son.

As long as the king is alive, the government remains intact.

We need to get out of here.

"What do we do now?" one of the girls asks as she steps up beside me.

It's Xandyr who answers. "We need to get to the forest," he says. "Regroup. I know a place where we can hide out."

"But my son..."

Helena's eyes are red. She is terrified.

I step close and put my hands on her shoulders. "We'll find him," I say. "But we need to find a place to hole up while we make plans."

She looks like she wants to protest. But she's an intelligent woman. She has to be, to have survived this long.

To keep me alive.

She doesn't protest as I lead our small group of survivors from the ruins of the palace. Outside I see movement in the palace grounds for the first time, at the far end of the building. Palace staff? Guards?

But they're dressed in ragged clothing, not uniforms.

And each of the half-dozen has a red cloth tied around their heads.

Red Bloods.

Rebels.

Have they been here in Mag City this whole time? In the palace?

They're about fifty yards away, heading off into the gardens. They must have stayed to see if their bombs accomplished their goal. To destroy the entire structure of Elleon's government. We're on the same side, after all.

One looks back, swinging a plasma rifle to cover their retreat. I freeze, unable to move. Our eyes meet, the Red Blood rebel and me. I'd recognize her anywhere.

Ulna.

"C'mon!" another Red Blood shouts at her as she stands there staring at me. I look at the others then. And find I recognize two more.

My brother Hern, hands tied in front of him, is being pushed along by his captors. They must have killed his guards and took him prisoner.

The other is River.

River! Is it really him? But—

I drop to my knees, unable to process this.

River is alive. And he's with the Red Blood rebels.

All of this has been a lie.

Through the foliage of the gardens, I see a truck pull up behind him, running over flower borders and uprooting shrubbery. The Red Bloods pile in and the doors slam behind them.

And my one thought as the truck disappears is that I can never trust my own perceptions again.

I have been manipulated by a master.

King Ilan. My father.

I can trust nothing. No one. Not even myself.

Especially not myself.

About Author

Laren Ruby

She is a self-proclaimed book nerd who lives in Alabama with her husband, 4 Boxer fur-kids, cat, turtle, and a tortoise. She also has 3 ducks and 8 chickens. When she's not feeding her farm, she loves to write. She loves adding books to her shelf. One of her absolute dreams is to have an in-home library with a rolling ladder. Because, why not?

What does she do for fun? She has watched every episode of Forensic Files. She's crime show obsessed. Anything in podcasts, movies, tv. Outside of that, she believes that *Schitt's Creek* is absolute gold and uses quotes from the show daily.

She loves camping (not the tent kind), hiking, and fishing. Although she will read just about anything, her favorite is YA Dystopia and Sci-fi. Books and movies about the end of the world? Sign her up.

www.ingramcontent.com/pod-product-compliance
Lightning Source LLC
Chambersburg PA
CBHW020527310726
48979CB00014B/2236/J

* 9 7 8 1 7 3 7 9 7 1 1 0 8 *